the me you see

Shay Ray Stevens

This is a work of fiction.

All of the characters, organizations, and events

portrayed in this novel are either

products of the author's imagination or are used fictitiously.

❧

Copyright 2014 by Shay Ray Stevens

❧

ISBN: 978-1502402455

❧

❧

To those who have figured out who they are

apart from what people say they should be.

❧

Table of Contents

∼

the me you see

-Stefia-

I lay sprawled out on the stage with two bullets in my chest. Gurgling. Spitting. Gagging on blood. I couldn't swallow. I couldn't breathe. I stared up at the lights and fixated on the question of why no one had bothered to pull the curtain.

End of the show, folks.

But they didn't pull the curtain. They couldn't look away.

Carly held on for a minute. She had turned quickly when she saw the gun and was hit right in the ear. The bullet came with a pop and cracked its way through cartilage and bone and finally came to rest somewhere in the fleshy part of her head. I don't think she felt anything. There is comfort in that.

Erick was also shot in the head but from a different angle. It was nothing like in the movies. Death from a gunshot wound in real life is nothing like a gunshot wound on the big screen. Being shot in real life is somehow less dramatic. Bodies move differently. I guess it's something you can't fake for the camera.

Tony ran and was hit in the back. He fell forward, his chest slamming into the black wood of the stage floor while profanity sloshed out of his mouth. He gulped for air and died mid-inhale. I thought about Tony's younger brother, a master video gamer, and wondered if he'd be able to shoot the pixelated bad guys anymore without thinking about his oldest brother's very public demise.

A bullet caught Bobby's arm which spun him around. He pleaded and said, "Stop. You don't mean to do this. You don't want to…" The second bullet went right through his face; centered between his nose and left cheekbone. His cheekbones were so nice. It's how he got that modeling job with *Dinecktos*. They hadn't even had to airbrush him. I remember he had been pretty proud of that.

Aubrey hid behind the curtain and was shot three times. I don't know where she was hit but within seconds she had crumpled down and sat with her pretty white lace costume in a puddle of her own blood.

Then me, Stefia. Two in the chest, one in the head. Down I went, the last to go. There's no time to think when you're looking down the barrel of a gun. That whole life flashing

10

in front of your eyes thing? It's a total crock of shit. I'm telling you, there's no time to think about what you haven't done or should have done or want to do. There's no time for any of it.

I spit. I gurgled. I choked.

I died.

That's how it happened.

Everyone thinks that death is dramatic but really it's quick. It's so quick. It is done and over with and the people who are left alive hold on to that last convulsing messy breath, and that's what they remember. That's what sticks with them.

It's what they see.

It's like when you've got that dog that looks so pathetically ill and you can't decide whether or not to put it to sleep or let it hang on for one more day. And you finally decide that it's time to let the dog go and you take it in for its overdose of anesthesia and you sob and sob because he's taken his last breath. And you hold onto the hurt of those last minutes. How it was hard to breathe. How he was in so much pain. But really, the death isn't what hurts.

And maybe that's what I want people to know. Because people will worry and wonder and talk about it. It's not the death that hurts. It's all the stuff that leads up to it.

Actual death is quick.

We all think we are so protected. So careful. We think we take the right precautions to be safe. And yet the irony is that the things we need to worry about, we don't. We don't concern ourselves with the random things that blindside us on some stagnant Thursday in February. We don't care about things that we don't believe add up to the big picture.

But it all adds up. The little pieces make up the big one. And we are so unprotected.

He just happened to be there. He just happened to stand up and draw his gun. Did he even think about it? Did his day start out the same as any other and just happened to end with a gun in his hand?

Lubbock said what we see depends mainly on what we look for. And really, life is all about what we see. It's the visual. The presentation. That's how we take it in and figure out what's what.

In the end, we are only the stories that people tell about us.

This, then, is the story of me.

Or at least the me you see.

-Naomi-

It's quiet like death but smells like pancakes. I open my eyes and blink.

Once.

Twice.

Three times.

I think I hate this day.

I pull on yoga pants and the bright pink hoodie I'd hung on my doorknob the night before and schlep down the stairs. No one says anything when I enter the living room even though twelve people stand there. The room is so quiet and their thoughts so loud I can almost read them across their foreheads like a crawler on the bottom of a news screen.

Poor Naomi.

It's so sad.

What a shame.

Dad sits at the kitchen table with Aunt Melanie. They don't make eye contact. They don't talk. No one says anything.

No one ever says anything.

It turns out the pancake smell comes from freshly baked caramel rolls that the neighbors brought over because at times like this, people bake and bring it all to you because they don't know what else to do. We're supposed to eat the caramel rolls and chew our way through the sadness and frustration and wordless discomfort.

But no one touches the caramel rolls. No one says anything.

No one ever says anything.

To be fair, people often stay quiet simply because they don't know what to say. My sister Stefia never had that problem. I could depend on her to break the silence, to interject something funny or witty or intelligent. Stefia kept a multitude of words on the tip of her tongue, ready to aim a much needed phrase at just the right spot. Invariably, her remark was perfect and people always listened.

But then, that was Stefia. When she spoke, people gathered at her feet. My sister could have read the ingredients from a bar of soap and her audience would have proclaimed it to be the most magical thing they'd ever heard.

Stefia had been poured from of a tall glass of perfection; my mother's alluring beauty and my father's come-what-may disposition had been flawlessly combined into one person and offered to the rest of us as a gift. I always imagined that God had placed her in my mother's womb with a note that said, "A masterpiece. Enjoy."

But then the shooting happened, and she fell as though the walls of the Sistine Chapel itself had crumbled, leaving nothing but shattered fragments on a squalid floor.

So now we cry. We look at caramel rolls. And we tiptoe around a loss of words because the person who used to speak for all of us is no longer here.

**

I know that Things Happen. Kids get run over by cars. Houses catch on fire. Cars bust through ice and sink to the bottom of lakes. People get shot.

It's reality.

I know about reality. In reality, people leave and don't come back. I remember waking up four years ago when I was twelve and knowing in my heart that my mom was not coming home. We had piled her mail in the middle of the dining room table and one of the cats had jumped up while chasing a fly and knocked the pile over. No one picked it up.

That's how I knew she wasn't coming back. Because no one cared enough to pick up her mail.

Eventually mom's toppled pile of letters and bills grew into such a mess that we were actually kicking them around. People talk about having a giant elephant in the room— which generally can only be felt, not seen—but our giant elephant was physically manifested in a growing pile of mail.

After two weeks of tripping around mom's junk from the postal service, I suspected nothing had been added to the mountain in a while. A week later, I was positive no new envelopes addressed to her had been delivered to the house. I was old enough to realize mom was somewhere and had requested an address change. That was about the time dad yelled at us all to throw the pile away. So Stefia and Gabriella and I all tossed piece after piece of mail into a giant contractor's garbage bag and lugged it out to the trash can at the end of the driveway.

An elephant made up of an absent person's mail is heavy and hard to dump.

Dad sat all three of his girls down that night and said, "I don't know where your mom is. I don't know why she left. All I know is she's gone." Then he went out into the garage to work on his car, like he'd done nothing more than tell us the internet was down or the coffee pot was broken.

Gabriella pounded her fists into the beanbag chair she was on and cried. Then she flung obscenities that an eleven-year-old shouldn't know at the air dad had left when he walked out the front door. Stefia, almost fourteen, sat on the couch and stared blankly out the window at the huge tree in our front yard. I was twelve and figured the best thing I could do was leave the house and run down the sidewalk as far as it would take me. Because I was twelve, and I didn't know how to change what had just happened.

I haven't seen mom since I was twelve. I haven't heard from mom since I was twelve. I know she isn't anywhere around this town because people can't hide here. If you're in Granite Ledge, somebody knows where you are. And no one knows where my mom is.

I lean my back against the kitchen counter that holds the caramel rolls and wonder, does she know? Has my mom heard? Is she even still alive to attend her oldest daughter's funeral?

Oh. God. What if she shows up?

And what if she doesn't?

Dad says it doesn't matter either way. And maybe it doesn't. I'm all for reality but sometimes I think my dad is a total pacifist. Stefia called him Gandhi one time and he looked out the window at a chickadee in our bird bath and said, "One day, you will understand."

I keep looking for One Day on the calendar but it hasn't come up yet.

My mom should not have left, but she did. That's reality.

Someone should know where my mom is, but no one does. That's reality.

My sister is dead and mom probably doesn't even know.

And that's reality.

**

People will accuse me of painting over the past to say all the things everyone expects to hear after someone dies, but trust me when I tell you that I grew up believing that having Stefia as a sister was a promise that everything would be okay.

After mom left, life at home was a silent but swirling storm of disorder, and Stefia's sleight of hand kept me in the eye of that storm. She was my protector. My comedienne. The one who distracted me from the physical absence of a mother and the emotional absence of a father who either couldn't—or just plain wouldn't—say anything.

No one ever said anything. So Stefia had to.

And sweet Stefia, oh, the words that fell out of her mouth, the way she could make it all better. The simple manner in which she could twist her lips around a word and shape it into something useful. Something helpful. Something needed.

I remember countless late summer storms when the wind would howl and I would cower in the corner of my closet. There was no way she could have heard my whimpers over the bellowing of the wind, but Stefia would know I was scared and would come find me.

"Naomi. Naomi…" she'd call as she came down the hallway from her room to mine.

She was only a year older than me but decades braver, and she'd speak with the most soothing honey soaked voice, coating me with an impenetrable shell of protection.

"We're going to be okay, Naomi…"

God, I hated those storms. They'd whip up and turn the sky a shade of green black that made me think of the Wicked Witch from Oz. The wind would scream in competition with the sirens that served as its warning. It would roar against the house, pushing with a full-mouthed howl, threatening to collapse the walls and bury us within.

"Come out, Naomi. Come on."

But I couldn't. My legs would soften into useless rubbery pegs, unable to hold my weight, and I would shrink into the corner, concealed by hanging clothes and forgotten toys.

Then the closet door would squeak open and Stefia would crouch inside to find me huddled behind a mess of things.

She'd move whatever totes I had pulled around myself as a shelter and squish herself next to me.

"We're going to be okay. I promise."

She'd hold my hand, humming and singing; a warm pillar of strength next to my shaking body. But somehow, even though I trembled, I knew that if Stefia's words covered me, I was safe from the storm.

"See, Naomi? The storm is over. Everything is okay."

No matter what the angry sky tossed at our little house, I always survived. And I believed it was simply because Stefia said I would.

**

After mom left, people teased my father that with three daughters born within three years, his life would be one estrogen fueled disaster after another. They advised him to not get in the middle of the cat claws that were sure to fly between his girls. But that's really not how it was. Well, at least between two of the three of us.

It wasn't that Stefia played favorites, or that she only had enough love to pour out on one of us. I honestly believe even now that Stefia had enough love to fill up anything that breathed. So it wasn't that Stefia didn't adore or wasn't kind to Gabriella. It was that Gabriella didn't want kindness shown to her. Stefia had always chased after Gabriella, ending up in places I know she really would have rather not been, just to haul her sister out of trouble. Always. The scuffle down at the riverbank by Beidermann's. The car accident when Gabriella got her first minor consumption. Jimmy Kreeger's party. Stefia was there when dad couldn't be—when dad wouldn't be—like a sister and a parent and a friend all rolled into one.

Gabriella just didn't want anything to do with it.

I'd only seen Stefia cry a handful of times in my life. Most of them were because she couldn't reach someone who needed reaching. Most of the times, that person was Gabriella.

"I can't get to everyone. I get that," Stefia said to me one night. She and I were lying in the grass at Pine Tree Park, looking up to the sky for shooting stars that weren't there. "You'd think if I could affect someone from the stage, I could do the same with someone in real life."

I didn't say anything, mostly because I was one of those people who didn't know how to say things that wouldn't come easily. I didn't have the heart to tell her I really thought maybe there are some people who don't want to be reached.

And then, ironically enough, there are others who don't even realize they need to be.

**

I swipe my finger along the screen of my phone to unlock it and check my Facebook newsfeed. Normally I wouldn't think of looking at my phone in a room full of grieving, voiceless relatives because I was raised with manners. But since no one is talking to me or looking at me or even acknowledging that I'm still breathing even though my older sister isn't, no one will notice anyway.

Everything happens for a reason.

God never gives you more than you can handle.

He has a plan.

Praying for Granite Ledge.

The thing with Stefia was that even though she always knew what to say, it wasn't always what people wanted to hear. She could soothe you with her words, or she could set you straight. And it makes me wonder what Stefia would say in reply to the prayers and inspirational memes being posted today—the day of her funeral. I mean, is plastering some sympathetic words over a picture of a candle or a pristine snowy field supposed to help?

If Stefia were here, she'd compose something about how people post things to make themselves feel better about whatever has happened. Then she'd add that I should stop being so cynical.

I smirk at the thought.

I'm not a cynic, though. I'm a realist. By the end of next week, will anyone on Facebook remember what they are praying for? Will they even still be praying?

Aunt Melanie walks past me. She eyes the caramel rolls, and then turns towards me to look over my shoulder at the newsfeed I'm swiping through.

"Our thoughts are with the families of the victims of the Crystal Plains Theater Massacre," I say, mocking what I read from my phone. "Wait. Now it was a massacre?"

"Honey…" Aunt Melanie's voice trails off, unable to finish a sentence that she wasn't sure why she'd started.

"The death of six people is not a massacre," I say. "The Native Americans were massacred. The victims of the Holocaust were massacred. But the shooting at the theater?"

"Naomi," she says. "You of all people should know not to discredit the lives of the people who died at the theater…"

"I'm not discrediting anything. I just wish people would call it what it is."

She looks as though she has mixed pity and disgust in a bowl and painted it on her face. I hate the way she glares at me, like she wants me to believe she hasn't already made up her mind how to feel about my reactions.

I look away from her judgmental stare and wish for Stefia to be at my side. I wouldn't have to explain myself to Stefia.

Stefia would know what I meant. Stefia would be able to say it better.

Aunt Melanie didn't get it. Nobody did. I took a deep breath and remembered that Stefia told me once most people just need to talk and make noise to deal with what happens. They need to spout off words to sort out things they will never understand. It's just how most people cope.

The problem is noise doesn't ever change anything that's already happened.

Melanie offers a weak smile and turns from me to sit with dad. She mumbles something as she rests her hand on his shoulder. He doesn't look up. He doesn't say anything.

He never says anything.

**

Just three months ago on Christmas Eve, as Stefia and I hung stockings and lights on the banister of our open staircase, I cringed at Gabriella's empty stocking hook.

Gabriella, never happy in Granite Ledge, had dropped out of high school in October. In her quest to attain more than the black sheep status she'd earned here, she moved to Virginia with Adam, the supposed love of her life. Adam was nineteen and already a four time published author and he was going to rescue her from the dull life she led in small town Minnesota. Dad never even told her not to go.

Dad never said anything.

24

Bing Crosby's *White Christmas* played in the background while Stefia twisted strings of multicolored lights around the banister and into slats and out again, turning our home into a twinkling paradise heavy with the scent of pine and snickerdoodles.

She saw my eyes fall on the spot where Gabriella's stocking should have been hanging. I took a sip of hot apple cider, sucking the warm tartness across my tongue.

"You know," Stefia said, "human beings seem to have a big problem with how they view life experience."

"How so?"

"Well, most of them believe in the very bottom of their hearts that there is a way things should be."

I took another long sip of cider, the steam collecting on my cheeks and mixing with tears I wasn't fast enough to blink away.

"People want to believe there is some sort of equation for how life is supposed to go," she continued. "But you know what?"

"What?"

"That's bullshit, Naomi. There really isn't a way things should be. There's only what happens and what we do about it."

I stared hard at the hook that was supposed to hold Gabriella's stocking, remembering how years before I'd stared the same way at mom's empty hook.

"What happens, and what we do," she repeated, "is all there is."

**

I gawk at the caramel rolls. I'm hungry. But no one else is eating them; the pan stands like a glass display for looking but not touching.

No one would care if I ate one. No one would notice if I ate the whole pan. No one would even raise an eyebrow if I took all the rolls and threw them out into the snowbank. They'd just stare at me thinking, *Poor Naomi*, *It's so sad*, *What a shame*.

Oh, they would stare. But they wouldn't say a thing.

I decide against the rolls and walk back up the stairs, tracing my fingers along the banister and remembering how when Stefia, Gabriella, and I were all younger we dared each other to slide down the banister. None of us would ever do it, but we decided that sitting on our butts and bumping our way down the stairs would be safer and probably just as fun. So we'd run to the top of the stairs and bump our way back down, sometimes racing, sometimes crashing into each other at the bottom. We'd pull ourselves up from the rug, grabbing at the post with the swirly top that looked like a frosted cupcake, oblivious to the fact we were loosening it from the floor a bit more every time we pulled.

Those were fun times.

Dragging my toes along the carpet with each lazy step, I arrive at my bedroom closet. I slowly thumb through hangers trying to decide—but not caring about—what to drape over my body for the day. There will be media, there will be photographs taken and news footage shot. And I don't even care what I'm going to wear.

I could wear something from Stefia's room.

I could.

Even though she'd been blessed with the beauty in the family—God had placed all his eggs in one basket on that deal—Stefia and I had technically been able to wear the same size. We had always traded clothes back and forth. Always.

I knew that if Stefia were here, she'd have lent me anything I wanted to wear.

Of course, if Stefia were here, I wouldn't be going to a funeral.

Without even realizing I'd left my room, I find myself suddenly standing in front of Stefia's door and I hold my hand on the knob.

It's just Stefia's room.

It's just Stefia's room.

It's just...

Why can't I bring myself to turn the damn handle?

"What are you doing?" says a voice behind me, and I turn to see Aunt Melanie standing there with that look of pity and disgust. "Are you trying to get into Stefia's room?"

"You act like I'm breaking into something. It's just my sister's room."

"She's not here to tell you to stay out."

"She wouldn't if she were here. Stefia always let me come in."

"Well, the door is locked, so you can't get in anyway," Melanie says. "Your dad locked it the day after Stefia died. He was paranoid about the reporters. I thought you knew that."

I'd known Stefia's door was closed, but until now, I'd honestly not tried to get into her things. My hand was still resting on the doorknob, and I pushed the lever down just to prove to myself that Melanie wasn't lying.

"Didn't believe me?" she asks with a smirk when the lever doesn't move.

"The only person I ever believed is dead."

"Yeah. Well." Melanie shakes her head, tossing a look towards me that clearly conveys *you don't have to be so dramatic.*

I shoot her a look back that clearly conveys *you don't have to be such a bitch.*

"Honey," she starts aloud, "how are you doing? Has anyone talked to you about how you're feeling?"

Melanie works as an RN at the hospital. At some point she decided she wanted to go back to school as a psych major and she turned into the family shrink. It has always been mildly nauseating, even more so now that there is actually something psychologically distressing to discuss.

Or at least try to discuss. Because generally speaking, no one ever says anything.

"How are you, honey?" she repeats, as if changing the word she emphasizes will coerce me into answering.

I shrug my shoulders. My phone vibrates in the pocket of my hoodie with a text message. I decide against checking it.

"Naomi, you can be real with me," she says with the most plastic inflection I've yet heard from a human being. "Are you mad? Are you sad? Are you confused?"

I'm tired of her. I'm sixteen and she talks to me like I would talk to a puppy.

"Melanie, I just don't know. Okay? I'm not trying to hide anything. I think it is okay to simply not know how you feel when you're headed to your sister's funeral…"

"It's okay to be mad, Naomi," she says, making an effort to move closer to me and put her hand on my shoulder. "It's okay to be…"

If Stefia were here she would know what to say. If Stefia were here, she'd tell me how to respond. If Stefia were here…

…she'd tell me to speak up.

And then, as if Stefia is standing right behind me, cheering me on, I explode.

"Mad, Melanie?" I yell, smacking her hand away and slamming mine down on the railing. "Is that the best word you can come up with? Do you need a goddamn thesaurus?"

"Naomi," she says, sympathy washing from her face, "you don't need to yell."

"And sad? Yeah, that's a big word to explain how I'm feeling. Sure, Melanie. I'm sad."

My tone was suddenly mocking and sarcastic and Melanie wasn't sure how to respond. She looked down the stairway; I assumed to shoot some *Poor Naomi It's so sad what a shame* look to a concerned someone at the bottom of the stairs.

"Confused?" I continue. "Are we talking to two year olds? There are better words to explain this, Melanie! Mad is when you crack the screen on your phone. Confused is trying to figure out Algebra. But this? Come on, Melanie..."

"I wasn't trying to be condescending."

"How about trying to be fucking real?"

"Naomi!"

Aunt Melanie slaps her pink finger-tipped palm over her mouth, like she's never heard me curse before. In everyone's head I'm still seven-years-old with a missing front tooth and braids playing with My Little Pony dolls. They all want to know how I feel, but I think they want to hear it from a seven-year-old—with appropriate, easy to digest terms that can be dealt with simply and then ignored with a *run along and play* pat on the head.

Well, fuck. My sister died. Someone shot her on stage in a theater.

Fuck.

That's how I feel.

"I'm not sure what kind of answer you're looking for, Melanie," I continue, with quiet intensity. "I don't know how to explain how I feel after someone splattered my sister's brains all over the same stage she's been acting on for all these years. I don't know how to feel about that, Melanie."

Melanie quietly looks at the floor and moves her toe around inside her high heels.

"Do *you?*" I ask.

"I'm sorry," she finally says, shaking her head. "I'm really sorry you have to go through this."

My phone vibrates again and I know it's someone else asking how I feel. What they can do. How they can help. What they can bring. And I just don't know how to answer because no one has invented the words yet for how I am feeling. No one has written or spoken or even thought them up. Because those people who invent words only make up words to describe the feelings for things that are supposed to happen.

Not things like this.

Melanie turns carefully on her black shiny heels to head back down the stairs.

"Numb," I say, out of the blue.

"Excuse me?" Melanie stops on the stairs and turns back.

"Numb," I repeat. "I feel kind of numb."

She nods.

"I guess that makes sense," she says.

I want to tell Melanie that it doesn't matter to me if it makes sense or not. I wasn't saying anything to appease her, or anyone else for that matter. The only thing that really matters is what actually is. Because that's what Stefia always told me.

Perhaps I should put that up as a meme on Facebook. A picture of a tree or a sunset or a dog or a snow covered barn with the words *It is what it is.*

But your sister is dead, they will say. *Two shots to the chest and one to the head and she's dead. Don't you even care?*

I do care. I care more than anyone would understand. But it is what it is. And without a time machine or some magical wand, what's happened can't be changed.

And so we deal with what is.

And this is what is.

Melanie turns to walk back downstairs and I return to my closet. I choose a long black pencil skirt, a black shimmery tank, and a black sweater with sequins. Everything hangs on me. Nothing fits right anymore. I pull on black boots. Black hoops. I set a black hat on my strawberry blonde hair.

I can almost hear Stefia teasing me. I went through a phase awhile back when I would only wear black. Stefia would always shake her head and say *looks like you're headed to a funeral.*

Well...ha.

I don't mean funny ha.

I mean, ironic ha.

Headed to a funeral.

As put together as I'll ever be all day, I descend the stairs to find that everyone who was in the house before are already in their cars and steering out of the driveway. Dad is waiting for me in the car with Aunt Melanie.

I told them last night I could drive myself, but they wouldn't hear of it. They were too concerned with how I felt. How I was handling things.

It is what it is.

I adjust the waist of my skirt and check myself in the mirror before grabbing a coat to shield me from the chilly March air. Then I turn back.

The caramel rolls.

I backpedal into the kitchen and reach for the pan baked with love and given in discomfort. I wrap my fingers around one of the sticky, gooey rolls. The pan smells divine and I'm glad I remembered they were there. Because honestly, after a month of not eating more than a Kit Kat, a few dollar buns, and a slice of pizza, I'm hungry. And people need to stop ignoring how they feel.

And then they need to speak up.

-Shawn-

I remember when I found out my wife was dying.

It seems like just yesterday when Lindsey felt mostly fine, but a little dizzy. She waved it off as dehydration from our hiking trip. A week later the headaches began. Then she couldn't see out of her left eye.

"Maybe you should see a doctor," I suggested.

Cancer. That's such an ugly word. How do you get terminal cancer when you're 38? How is it that you're on a rock climbing adventure in June, and in July you're given six weeks to live?

Six weeks.

At first we pretended nothing was happening. I have no shame in admitting that because I know everyone lives with their own secret elephant that they completely ignore from time to time. Like, you know your elephant is there, because—let's face it—it's an elephant. But after a while, it's almost as if you no longer see it. You cling to some stupid idea that if you just close your eyes long enough, you can be powerful enough to wish it away.

After that stopped working, we did the same thing every couple with a terminal half does: we went around doing all the things we wished we would have done before we realized time is finite and runs out.

We went to a boys' choir concert at the mall, and a rainy, cold ball game at the new field with lights so bright they looked like spaceships descending upon us. She got her hair cut short and dyed it purple so it would look cool in case it started to fall out. She bought pieces for a quilt she'd never finish. She went to church. She sat up late eating pickled fish on crackers. She treated herself to giant mugs of full-fat hot cocoa.

One morning about four weeks after her diagnosis, she sat next to me with her fingers curled around my thigh and said, "I want to go see the play that my niece is in."

Normally, it wouldn't have been a big deal. Under any other circumstances, seeing a play would have been just one more adventure we attacked full force.

"I thought you hated the theater," I said. Like it mattered.

"I do," Lindsey responded, "but I love Stefia." Because it did matter.

Lindsey hadn't seen Stefia in almost four years. Drama sparked by the so-called *elective disappearance* of Stefia's mother—Lindsey's sister—had unintentionally mushroomed into a discomfort between everyone in Stefia's extended family. At first, no one knew what to say to Stefia or her sisters. And then, well…you know how it is. The longer you go without saying something, the less you have to say. And four years later, after no one has said anything, you realize how much those Elephants can mess things up without even trying.

"Okay," I said. "We'll go to the show."

And so I bought us tickets for *Taken by the Reigns* at the Crystal Plains Theater and we dressed up like we were seeing the President. I rented a tux and she wore a formal. It would be a night to remember. Everyone stared when we walked in but we didn't care. Because you just don't when you know that time is running out.

Now, I don't profess to know much about anything, least of all theater. The only play I'd ever been in was the Christmas pageant at church when I was six and I was so nervous I threw up all over the baby Jesus doll. So I don't know if the show we went to see was amazing or mediocre or what. It didn't matter. What I do know is that the show made my wife happy, and that was worth ten times the cost of the tickets. She smiled. She laughed.

My wife was happy.

Driving home that night, Lindsey said, "You know, most of the time I was watching the show, I forgot I was even watching someone I knew."

"Yeah?"

"Yeah. And I think that's how you know someone is a good actor. If they can make you forget that you know them. That you're not watching them thinking *oh, I'd better say they did a good job because otherwise Christmas will be uncomfortable.* You actually want to tell them they did a great job because they really did."

We hadn't celebrated Christmas with Stefia's family for almost four years, and I knew that had cut Lindsey's insides apart. Elephants are destructive, you know; their tusks pointy and sharp.

As the days went on, my wife grew quieter. She still smiled and her health seemed to be good relatively speaking, but it seemed like Lindsey was talking less. Growing more introspective. Perhaps contemplating what was to come.

One night I lay down next to her in bed as she shook. I panicked. I thought *oh god this is the end, this is really it. She's been doing so good and now I'm going to lose her.* But then I realized she was shaking because she was crying.

"What's wrong?" I asked and brushed the pad of my thumb under her eye to wipe away a tear.

She sniffled and then coughed and when she recovered said she couldn't decide if she was angry or sad.

"What about?"

"Wasted time."

I held her and she blew deep puffs of air at my chest, hiccoughing on tears and snot as they came faster.

"She looked so happy," she said finally.

"Who?"

"Stefia."

"What?"

"On stage. She looked so happy."

I didn't know if we'd started a new conversation or if Stefia on stage somehow tied into wasted time so I listened before commenting because words are so precious when you know time is running out.

"She's doing what she loves," she continued. "She hasn't wasted time."

A frenzy of ice sloshed through my veins. Had we reached the part where my wife would come clean and admit she had hated everything about our life together? Would she walk to the closet and collect her things before she danced out to a life that didn't feel wasted?

She didn't.

"I want to see the show again," Lindsey said. "I need to see it again."

The final performance of the show was the following night. It also happened to be completely sold out, but I mentioned something to the box office manager about "being family" and "six weeks to live." I thanked him profusely when he said they would set up two additional chairs off an aisle and make room.

"Can I ask one other favor?" I said.

"Anything," he responded.

"Don't tell Stefia about this, okay?"

I could almost hear his wink over the phone, like he was happy to keep our little secret.

When you see a play more than once, you pick out things you didn't get the first time. So when we saw it again, I paid much closer attention. Our seats had been added to the end of the third row and we were so close I could see the spray of spit from lines delivered, the bubbles of sweat collecting as the spotlight warmed Stefia's skin. Sitting so close to the stage sucked me further into Stefia's world of make-believe, further and further until the boundaries between actor and audience blurred and I felt as though I'd been pulled from chair and wrapped around her feet.

What my wife had said was true—Stefia really was the brightest star on that stage.

When the performance was over, the cast members bounced their post-show adrenalized selves into the lobby. They set themselves against the wall like a receiving line at a wedding, shaking hands and accepting accolades from their adoring fans.

So glad you enjoyed the performance!

Thanks for coming!

You're too kind, really. I just enjoy being on stage.

I thought we were going to blast past the niceties of the actor line, like we had the first time we'd seen the show, but Lindsey grabbed me by the arm.

"I need to say something to her. I just need to say…"

"Say what?"

"Something."

It was so not like my wife to have to say anything. She was a master at letting things lie. But things are different when time is finite and suddenly you find that your mouth has filled up with all the things you never got to say.

We waited in line through all the congratulations, well dones, and good jobs, shaking hands with the fifteen actors who had poured themselves out on stage for the last two hours. Since Stefia was one of the leads, she was towards the end of the line. So my wife waited. And waited.

"Are you getting tired?" I asked after a few minutes. "Do you want to sit?"

"No," she said and shook her head. "I just need to say something to her."

And just like that, it happened. The line shuffled ahead and they were standing right in front of each other.

It's funny how the elephant never really goes away, you know? Four years of discomfort passed between the two of them in a glance that took less than a second. It was all there in that look, the mixture of surprise and disbelief and *oh my god what do I say?*

Stefia refocused with a swallow and squared her shoulders.

"Aunt Lindsey," she said, with emotion that wasn't easily named. "How nice of you to come to the show."

"I just need to say something," Lindsey continued. "Hear me out."

Lindsey grabbed Stefia's hands and stared into her eyes with a severity I was noticing more often as her time on earth ticked away.

"Okay…" Stefia said, oddly uncomfortable with the attention.

"Stefia, you are talented. You are so talented, baby girl. You are like…a hidden pocket of glitter."

"Oh, Lindsey…"

"No, please let me finish. You shine up there on stage like those lights at the softball field. The ones that let you see for miles around? That's you, Stefia. You are showing people their way. Don't ever stop doing this. You're amazing."

Stefia was starting to blush, which I didn't understand because Lindsey wasn't telling her anything different than what the hundred people before her in line had said. But she squeezed at Lindsey's hands and politely said, "Thank you, Lindsey. Thank you for coming."

"There's one more thing I need to tell you," Lindsey said, cutting her off.

I saw my wife look down at floor, then sigh and close her eyes. After a moment, she opened them back up and looked straight into Stefia's eyes for the second time.

"You, sweet Stefia," she said, "you are nothing like your mother. And don't ever let anyone tell you differently."

For a second, a seriousness pulsed between them; a connection that tied them up in something I couldn't see. Then Stefia's lips warmed into a smile that spread slowly across her face as she pulled Lindsey in for a hug.

"Thank you, Lindsey," she whispered into my wife's ear. "Thank you for coming."

And it somehow seemed to me that the second time Stefia said it, she meant something entirely different than the first.

**

Immediately after seeing the second show, my wife completely fixated on Stefia. Not really Stefia the person, because we didn't ever see her again. It was more the idea of Stefia that my wife was hyper-focused on. It was as if because Stefia did what she wanted and took things the direction she chose to go, it inspired my wife to do even more in her last days. And as we passed that six weeks to live mark and headed into eight weeks, ten weeks, three months, five months, I found myself thankful that we had sat in the audience watching Stefia paint her magical pictures that my wife interpreted as *everyone can be happy if they just follow their dreams.*

Stefia was the inspiration. She aroused the need for my wife to continue. She sparked an interest in daily life and made my wife look at everything from the simple to the infinitely complex to everything in between and figure out what she loved. My wife grew to believe more each day that doing what she loved was important not because she was dying, but because she was still alive.

My wife told me she wanted to drive a car with the top down to someplace she'd never been before. She wanted to take an old rusted out baby blue farm truck, find a deserted intersection where two gravel roads come together, and make love right there. She wanted to visit a city so big we had to take a taxi to get around and then she wanted to tip the driver with a hundred dollar bill. Just because she could. Because she wanted to. Because it was something she loved.

She bought a croton house plant and transplanted it into a piece of pottery she fashioned with her own sweet hands. She stopped drinking coffee and started drinking chai tea. She painted her nails a different color every single day. She volunteered at a women's shelter. She shopped for Christmas three months early. She celebrated Hanukah. She wrote poems. She baked rye bread. She used china and gold plated silverware to eat peanut butter and jelly.

And I watched her in wonder. I watched as she spun around in a mad frenzy, doing all the things she had always wanted to do, wondering why had she waited? Why had she wasted so much time before?

And then I wondered the same thing of myself.

Was I waiting?

Had I wasted time?

Was I doing what I loved?

I wondered.

Things look different when you are contemplating the end. And I spent a lot of time wondering if it was easier to be at the end knowing you had time to think on it, or if it was harder to deal with if it snuck up on you suddenly.

One night we sat in the warmth of conversation and a fireplace, celebrating what would have seemed to most people to be the very least of things. We'd had a bottle of wine between the two of us—mostly me, because she couldn't handle it well—and she told me to stop being so whiny about life.

"I'm doing the things I've always wanted to do," she said. "I'm crossing everything off my bucket list." Then she took another sip of her wine. She was gorgeous and tipsy and I loved her more than anything and everything in the world.

"What will I do when I run out of things to do?" she said with just a hint of a happy slur. "I'll tell you what I'll do. When I run out of things on my bucket list, I'll kick the bucket!"

She held her wine glass up and toasted to the winter sky outside our bay window, tossing back what was left in the glass.

"When I die," she said, setting the wine glass next to her, "don't write an obituary for me."

"What?"

"Obituaries are all the same. They're like a written participation ribbon for having shown up and breathed. It's all the same phrases. *She loved her family* or *she was a light to those around her.* Nice, neat phrases. Like…a brassy ribbon tied around an existence that might or might not have been worth the space and air it took up."

"Don't talk like that," I said.

"Like what?" she said. The wine had filled her with cynicism by the bucketful and she had grown weary of hiding anything that should have stayed hidden. "Let's not pretend. It doesn't help anything."

She'd lost so much weight and yet her face was puffy from all the medication she was on.

"I'm not pretending," I said. "But it doesn't help anything to keep pointing it out either."

"You know, Shawn," she said, "you could be worse off than me."

"What?"

"Here I'm trying to get through this bucket list before I kick it because I know the end is coming. You…you could die in a car crash tomorrow. You could die suddenly without even knowing what your bucket list is."

There was something eerie about her words, something strange about her even bringing it up. And I didn't like thinking about it because she was telling the god's honest truth.

"I am doing everything right now that would be on my bucket list if I had one," I said.

"Like what? Watching your dying wife get drunk?"

"No. Just spending time with the person I love more than anything in the whole world."

I would have stayed there watching her for forever. I just couldn't suck in enough of her. I felt like I spent every day wildly running after her with a cup, trying to catch the overflow of who she was before there was no more of her to catch.

"Things look different when days are numbered," I finally said.

"They shouldn't."

I knew she was right. I knew we weren't supposed to save things for looking different or mattering for when the reality of finite days punched through our skull. But it seemed to be one of the more stupid human tricks we were all guilty of performing.

"I love you," I said. The wine and the soft crackle of the cedar log in the fireplace made everything about me warm and tingly, even my eyeballs and the tips of my fingers. "I have always loved you."

She looked so small and insignificant in her rocking chair, the quilt around her seeming to swallow her whole. But she beamed and sparkled with a glittery light on her upturned lips as her eyelids grew heavy and she inched closer to sleep.

"I have always known that," she said. "Always."

**

I dreamed last night of heaven. I woke up in a brilliant fog and tried to sketch what I had seen: a silver blue sky with cedar trees the color of warmth lining a gravel path that rounded into a gentle bend. Just enough that you couldn't see around the corner. But you knew what was coming: pure brilliant beauty.

In the dream, my wife was standing on the path. I couldn't see her as a solid thing and yet I knew she was there. In my wakened state, I furiously tried to sketch a figure that wasn't really a figure. I tried to sketch the liquid fluid notes of her voice that had come out as ribbons of shimmering silk when she spoke. I tried to sketch it all, everything I had seen. Because in the dream, it was beautiful. In the dream, it was peaceful.

I tried to sketch it all.

Because it was beautiful.

But today is different. Today is not beautiful. Today I'm going to a funeral.

My wife sits on the edge of the bed, hardly able to put weight on her legs or keep balance, not just because she's gotten weaker in the last month, but also because she can't process what happened.

Like any of us could.

"I don't get it," she says, as I help get her dressed. Her arms are flaccid and she doesn't want to move. "I don't get what happened. It doesn't make sense. She was doing what she loved."

I can't even respond because it feels like I've swallowed a handful of cotton balls and if I open my mouth to speak I'll gag. I can't agree or disagree. I just don't know.

"She was doing what she loved," my wife says again.

I nod.

I slip my wife's arm into the sleeve of her coat and think about her niece. How she was doing what she loved because it was what she loved and not because she thought it made a difference to anyone or anything. It was just what she loved. If I could have picked Stefia up off that stage and shook her alive I would have told her that what she did mattered. It had always mattered. She had affected people she didn't even realize she had affected. She had been the topics of people's conversation when they were at the end of their rope and needed something to hang on to.

And maybe, just maybe, she had even helped to keep them alive.

"She was just doing what she loved," my wife repeats again like a mantra that can't be forgotten, her face sick with confusion and pale with incredulity. "Just what she loved."

I nod again.

"I've been doing what I loved," she says.

And I nod, but this time more slowly and every bob of my head feels like a weight pulling my chin closer to the ground. Because I know what thoughts my wife has connected. And I get what she's saying.

And I have to accept it.

I have to.

We don't say anything else. My wife leans on me to stand up and I help her with slow footsteps to an exit that neither of us knows how to handle.

-Heidi-

Lullaby, and good night...

A lullaby plays over the loudspeaker system whenever a
baby is born here. I love to hear that sound. Another life
successfully brought into the world. A potential bright spot
on the pockmarked face of our country's population.

I work as a labor and delivery nurse and I love my job. I
love meeting the people. I love how different they all are. I
love their stories. But mostly I love their vision. Their
carefully laid out plans for how they're going to raise the
baby they've just birthed to be the Person Who Changes
The World. They're not going to make the same mistakes
their parents made. They're going to do things differently.
Because they are different.

They say it's all in how you're raised, you know? It's all about what your parents did or didn't do or how many siblings you had or what kind of neighborhood you grew up in or if you sold Girl Scout cookies or let the JWs into your house. What kind of food you ate for dinner. If you sat at the dinner table as a family or ate in front of the television. How early you ate eggs or peanuts and how much candy your parents allowed you to have.

Let me tell you what I think: it's all a big joke. And I've only found one person who ever agreed with me.

Stefia.

I've worked on this floor for almost 20 years. It never fails to amaze me how much the birthing and parenting recommendations change year to year. What new theories they come up with. What practices aren't okay today that were okay yesterday. What beliefs are going to mess your baby up for good, and what things don't make a difference at all.

"Heidi?" my co-worker, Amanda, asks. She is fresh out of nursing school and makes me crazy. Her squeaky voice is the solitary reason I eat too much chocolate when my shift is done.

"Yeah?"

"The patient in room 310 is asking for more ice chips."

"So give her more ice chips."

"Do you think that's okay, though? She's had, like, twenty-four cups or something of ice since she got here."

"It's just ice, Amanda. Frozen water. It's not going to kill anyone."

That is, unless there was some new study about laboring mothers and ice that I missed the memo on.

Amanda turns around and leaves quickly with the twenty-fifth cup of ice, looking like a puppy that has been yelled at. I think about apologizing for about half a second but decide against it. That girl drives me crazy just by breathing.

Maryanne, the charge nurse, shoots me a look that I can't quite read. I can't tell if she thinks I should follow Amanda to apologize, or if she thinks Amanda is annoying, too. Maybe she just knows that I'm on edge because Stefia is being buried today and I'm stuck here with Miss Ice Chip. And honestly, that's just about enough to make me want to drink about a quart of whatever they shoot in your spine for an epidural.

Numb me up and make me stupid so I can totally forget this day even happened.

I shuffle papers on the desk at the nurse's station, making a mental note of what rooms are full and who is closest to delivering. Room 310 is closest but wants to go au natural and refuses to let her labor be augmented unless there is a medical emergency. Room 307 is a good four hours from delivery and would literally do anything to speed it up.

Room 303 has a whole list of things she wants after the baby arrives.

The mothers are all so needy. And so worried. And it makes me wonder when it was that things got so complicated. Birth is just birth. It's the same process as it was a thousand years ago. Babies are still just babies and they need to eat and sleep. Why do we complicate things?

The hard stuff comes after the birth. Most women don't want to hear about that while they're trying to push their baby out, but I think on some level they know it's true. The hard stuff comes later. But it's not even the stuff that new parents think is going to be hard. Not all the stuff that people talk about or read about or research while they're decorating the nursery or deciding whether or not to vaccinate. It's the stuff that no one is brave enough to talk about.

I contemplate what kind of parent Miss Ice Chip would be. She's a total flake. To be honest, I'm not even sure how she got hired except for maybe her sparkling bedside manner. She makes most patients smile, and she's calm and peaceful—perfect for those new age hippy mothers who come in and think that low lighting and soft music will change anything about how their babies come into the world. But as a nurse, as someone who needs brains to complete a task, she's a shame to the department.

Amanda as a parent would be hilarious.

Except that's the thing people don't get. I've watched hundreds of women walk out of the hospital with babies, bringing them home to raise them up the right way. They've all got different ideas about what that is, though. They've all read different books, followed different baby gurus on Twitter, and liked a multitude of conflicting baby-raising things on Facebook. But what they don't get is that it doesn't matter.

It really doesn't.

Or I should say it has no bearing on how your kid turns out. It has no bearing on how their life ends up. And no one wants to talk about that because it makes parenting seem worthless. If a child's life is going to turn out how it turns out, why do we all try so hard? Why do we debate babywearing and vaccination and whether or not a child should be breastfed for five weeks or five years?

Does it matter?

No one wants to contemplate the answers to these questions because if there's any truth to them, then a parent's job is pretty worthless. And who wants to be the bearer of that message? Who wants to be the one to point out that if you offer a golden platter of Everything Perfect to two different kids, they might each take that platter in opposite directions? One might cure cancer while the other invents a new kind of atomic bomb and purposely blows up three quarters of the world.

How much of what we do even matters?

I don't know if any of it does.

And neither did Stefia.

**

I talked to Stefia for the last time a little over a month ago. Of course I didn't know it would be the last time. It's funny, I always think if I would have known it was the last time I was going to talk to someone, I would have said something different—awe inspiring or infinitely humorous. But we can't ever know it's the last time. That's the way it works.

And maybe it's better that way.

I had walked into the coffee shop for my Americano before my Tuesday shift (like always) and she was there (like always). She asked if I wanted room for cream, and like always, I refused.

Stefia was one of those beautiful and friendly and smart people, a mix of things that everyone would write down on their Personality Wish List if ever they were given the option. She could hold her own in conversation on just about every topic I'd ever brought up, which was quite a few, since my visits usually fell smack in the middle of the dead time at the coffee shop.

"What's on your mind today?" she asked, as she pressed the lid over the to-go cup and handed it across the counter to me.

I took the cup, removed the lid (like always), and blew gently into the glorious bean water that would fuel my ten hour shift.

"I'm thinking about parents," I answered.

"New parents? Old parents?" she asked. "Are you having another baby?"

I laughed. "God, no. My two are finally grown up and moved away. I'd die if I had to go through labor at my age."

"You're not that old," Stefia said.

"Seriously, 42 is too old for labor," I said, putting a definite punctuation mark on the entire idea.

Stefia came around the counter and joined me on the customer side of the shop, filling her own mustard colored mug from the air pot on the center island. She leaned against the granite slab, sipping her dark hazelnut blend (like always) and waited for me to speak.

"Do you think parents matter?" I asked her.

She looked down at her feet and I could tell she was wiggling her toes around in the fronts of the moccasins she wore around the shop.

"That's kind of a loaded question," she answered.

"Do you think how a parent raises their child makes any difference in a child's life?"

"There are a lot of things that make a difference in a child's life," Stefia said. "Not just the parents. Maybe not the parents at all."

"It has to make some difference, doesn't it?"

"Why? Maybe it doesn't have anything to do with how you were raised."

"It has to play some part," I said.

"Not always. Why do some kids play violent video games and not go crazy, but others play the same game and shoot up their school?"

"I don't know," I said. And then with a sigh that spoke more than my words, added, "I just don't know anymore."

"What's really going on?" she asked. "What are you actually talking about?"

All I needed was an invitation and it came spewing out of my mouth. I told her about the phone call I'd received two nights earlier and how my 19 year old son was in jail for possession for the third time. And his girlfriend was pregnant but she'd lost the baby when he pushed her down the stairs.

"He wasn't raised that way," I said. "I mean, my husband and I are so far from that world…it's like, how did he end up there? You believe me, right?"

"People always want to blame the parents," she said, without skipping a beat.

"Well, what else is there?"

She took a chair at the table I was at, her thin and toned body like a trophy of youth she wouldn't appreciate until she was older. And I wondered suddenly why I was discussing any of my issues with her. A solid twenty years— at least—separated us. Why did her opinion even matter to me?

"Parents aren't the be-all, end-all of influence," she continued with a shrug. "Sometimes, what influences someone is just random."

"Random," I repeated, practically choking on the word. "What about your parents? They've influenced you, right?"

Stefia sat with her elbows resting on the table, hands holding her cup just under chin, but she didn't drink.

"My mom isn't around. Hasn't been for several years. My dad is just barely getting by with mom gone, even all this time later. He's like some corn husk that was tossed on the ground to wither away."

"I'm sorry. I didn't know she had died."

"She didn't. She left."

Stefia wound her right foot around the leg of her chair, slipping her moccasin off and on, off and on.

"Where do you get your support?" I asked. "I mean, if your mom is gone and your dad is…"

"…completely detached?"

"Yeah. Where was your support? Who raised you up?"

Stefia set her mug down and pushed her thumb back and forth across the side of it like she was trying to rub off a stain.

"The theater," she said.

She kept rubbing at that spot on her mug. I was pretty sure it was a flaw in the ceramic but she was determined to rub it out.

"So…you've been raised and had all your support from…a stage?"

"Not just the stage," she said, giving up on the spot and picking up the mug to take a short but thoughtful sip. "The theater isn't just a stage. It's people and…an energy. I've been raised by those who have watched me. And by people I've watched. I see a lot from up on stage. The audience speaks volumes without saying a word."

Then she smiled at me.

"Don't let your son get you down," she continued. "Kids screw up. It's what we do."

I let out a sarcastic snort and picked up my mug.

"I don't believe that you, Stefia, even possess the capability to screw up."

She looked at me with a slightly crooked smile that I didn't think could possibly show up on her pretty face.

"Oh, Heidi," she said, taking a slow sip of what was left in her mug. "You would be surprised."

**

A week later, after talking a teen mom-to-be through an epidural, Amanda caught me in the hallway by the arm.

"Oh my god, did you hear?"

She pulled me into an alcove, twisting my arm as she yanked me further into the corner. I opened my mouth to yell at her but when our eyes met, I realized her face had lost all color except for a mascara streak on her cheek.

"There was a shooting...at the theater...just twenty minutes ago. Oh my god..."

It spilled out of her mouth in between gasps that got more shallow every time she tried to speak.

"Amanda, slow down. Take a breath."

"There was a goddamn shooting!" she yelled. "At the theater!"

"What theater?" I yelled back, assuming she meant one of the three movie theaters near the hospital.

"The Crystal Plains Theater."

Amanda leaned against the wall and then slumped down until she sat on the floor. Immediately the questions spun through my head: how many people were dead? Was the shooting inside? Outside? Did the shooter aim at the audience? The actors on stage?

Oh. God.

Maryanne stuck her head around the corner of the alcove. She looked at Amanda, who stared blankly at the carpet with tears dripping off her chin.

"Pull yourself together," Maryann hissed at Amanda. "If you're going to freak out, do it in the nurse's lounge."

Then Maryanne looked to me.

"Room 317 is ready to deliver. I need you."

I nodded on complete autopilot, following Maryanne and passing through the door of 317 to assist with the chaos of birth. I encouraged and instructed and as I did my job, realized there was something uncomfortably disjointed about helping to deliver a baby and, at the same time, waiting on the names of the dead.

Life is kind of strange that way.

Eight hours later as the sun was just coming up, I walked out of the hospital. I stood on the sidewalk, using my phone to stream live video of the press conference about the shooting. My hands shook as I waited. The police chief wasn't talking fast enough. They weren't...

When they read Stefia's name, my cell phone dropped from my hand and hit the sidewalk, the screen shattering.

It couldn't be. It just couldn't.

I collapsed to my knees, the cold of the sidewalk biting through my scrubs. A guy in a puffy orange jacket who was walking past stopped and bent down to help me up.

"Hey lady, lady...are you okay?" he said. "Did you fall? Do you need help?"

I shook my head, staring at the concrete I was kneeling on.

"Lady, are you okay?"

I was not okay.

I was not okay.

**

Amanda grabs Ice Cup Number Twenty-Six for room 310.

"This woman is going to be in labor forever," she says, rolling her eyes. "Why doesn't she just let the doctor break her water?"

I don't answer. I don't look at her. I just stare at the computer screen and pretend I'm entering chart information.

"Listen," she continues, quieter. "I know you're having a rough day. I know this day sucks for you."

Amanda touches my shoulder.

"I'm sorry you had to work."

I look up at her to see a hesitant smile, like she almost thinks I'm going to smack her for touching me.

"You should probably go deliver that ice before it melts," I say.

She turns to head to room 310 and I'm positive that any personality flaw that irks me about her has little, if anything, to do with how she was raised. Annoying is just what Amanda is—maybe for some completely random reason that will never be known.

I think about all those people that died. Did any of their parents look into their future and see it coming?

Of course not.

I wanted to bust in on all the laboring women and tell them to stop the bickering back and forth about vaccinations and babywearing and breastfeeding and whether a kid should sleep on their stomach or back or side or hanging from their feet because it doesn't really matter in the end, does it? We deliver all these babies into sterile, crisp white rooms only to release them into a world of piled up shit.

It really doesn't matter what we do.

You don't plan in the end that your kids' dreams are going to get cut short. You don't plan your kid is going to end up lying dead on the stage of a theater in a small town.

All those parents of the young people who died... did they know that when they were discussing the differences on the pros and cons of circumcision or whether or not the mom should work outside the home that their kid was going to end up shot on some random Thursday?

Of course not.

I keep thinking about that. I keep thinking on all the new parents and middle aged parents and older parents who walk around saying *not my kid*. That will never happen to *my* kid. As in just by saying that, you have some kind of guarantee that your kid will turn out perfect.

Saying it is true does not make it true. Why don't they get it?

There are jails full of people's kids to prove it. My kid is one of them. You can't tell me that every cell is taken up by someone whose parents were complete screw ups. Because I'm not a screw up.

Birth is a predictable process. Sperm meets egg. Egg divides a bazillion times. Fetus matures. If there are no complications, birth happens and the proud parents take home their latest tax deduction.

Parenting, however, is not predictable. Parenting is not a mathematical equation. You can do A plus B and think you're going to get C, but you might actually end up with the equivalent of Z in a completely different language. You can give your kids everything the latest child psychologist guru says they should have and serve it up to them in a sparkling bucket of happy, and your kid might take the bucket, tip it over, set it on fire, and walk the other way.

And no one knows why.

Anyone's kid could have been at that theater in that mess that happened. Anyone's kid could have been in the audience, hiding and screaming or trying to run. Anyone's kid could have been on stage getting shot at.

You don't think so? How in the world can any honest parent answer no?

So. Does it really matter how you are raised?

I just don't know anymore.

Lullaby, and good night…

I love that sound. I love when that lullaby plays over the loudspeaker. Because with another new life, there is the hope of a bright spot on the pockmarked face of humanity.

There is hope, but no guarantee.

-Niles-

Their house was the same shade of blue as my first wife's eyes; almost one of those colors you shouldn't paint the exterior of a house. That piercing shade of blue was the entire reason I initially looked across the street and stared at Stefia.

I moved into the Dutch Colonial across from Stefia four years ago. It had been vacant for a year before I took it over, so there was work to be done. I got it for a steal and immediately went to work, first repairing, and then molding it into the spot of refuge I'd bought it to be.

I had assumed that shortly after my work began, the neighborhood welcome wagon would show up. I imagined there would be plates of cookies and offers to help with whatever was needed. That's how we would have done it where I grew up. But that wasn't how they did it in Minnesota. Oh, sure, I knew neighbors were peeking from behind curtains, wondering who the late 40ish guy was who had taken up residence in that Dutch Colonial with the peeling white paint. And admittedly, there were a few that were brave enough to walk by and wave. But as far as being neighborly, as far as offering help…well, that whole Minnesota Nice thing seemed to be a thing made of fairy tales, or at the very least, greatly exaggerated.

I didn't really know much about small towns in Minnesota. And they didn't know much about me. And maybe that was the whole problem.

Two weeks after I had moved in, I thought I might make a good impression by being my own reverse welcome wagon. I baked a plate of cookies and planned to walk right over to that house that was the same shade of blue as my first wife's eyes.

Why that house? Why not any of the others on the street?

It had as much to do with the shade of the paint that stuck to its walls as it did with the beautiful girl who often sat under the tree in its front yard.

I know what you're thinking. You're thinking: *Niles, stop it. I don't want to hear it. You have to know it was wrong.*

I know you're thinking I'm a bad person, but I couldn't stop. And you wouldn't think it was wrong if you understood what was happening.

I arranged two dozen Russian teacakes on a beautiful burnt orange platter and carried it across the street. Stefia was sitting at the base of the tree, like she'd done most days since I'd moved in. She was pawing slowly through the leaves on the ground like she was searching for something lost.

She was so beautiful. Long and thin like a stick of taffy you'd held in one hand and stretched out with your teeth. Her skin was creamy and white like a vanilla pudding pop.

Oh. God.

"Hello," I said.

I figured she would have heard my footsteps crunching into the leaves, but she was so engrossed in her search that she jumped when I spoke.

"I'm sorry to frighten you," I said, putting my hand out to calm her frantic stare. "I was on my way over here to introduce myself and deliver these cookies. I noticed you seem to be looking for something. Do you need help?"

When I really looked, I saw tears in her eyes. She wiped them away, embarrassed to have a stranger see her crying.

"No, that's okay," she said, remaining seated in the leaves. "I'm okay. I found what I was looking for."

I looked in her lap and saw she was holding a crudely made wooden box with bits and pieces of stuff inside. She fingered at a piece of pink lined paper in her hand, a note obviously scribbled on it. She folded up the paper and shoved it back inside the box.

"Are you sure you're okay?"

"Yes. I'm fine. Are you the new neighbor from across the street?"

"Yes," I said. "I just moved in a couple weeks ago. With moving in and all the repairs, I haven't had a chance to make a proper introduction. I'm Niles Connelly."

I handed her the cookies, which she took with a smile and set down next to the box of treasures.

I extended my hand for her to shake.

"And you are?" I prompted.

She took my hand to shake it and I pulled her up into a standing position.

"Thanks," she said. "I'm Stefia."

"Stefia. Now that's a lovely name."

"That's what everyone says." She smiled, cautiously.

"I rather like it."

"I hate it," she confessed. "I'd much rather have a normal name. Like Mary. Or Sue."

"I think you look like a Stefia," I said. "Far too pretty to have a normal name."

She blushed.

"In fact," I continued, "I think Stefia is a name that just screams someone destined for great things."

"I was told it is a cross between Stephanie which means crown and Sophia which means wisdom."

"Interesting cross of names," I pondered. "Why the combination?"

"Because my father wanted his first born daughter to be named Stephanie and my mother was rooting for Sophia."

"Ah," I said. "I guess I would I tend to side with your mother."

"I don't," she said quickly.

"Oh?" I said, wondering why the abrupt dismissal.

"She's not here. I mean, my mom."

"Gone for the afternoon?"

"No. Gone forever."

"I'm sorry," I said, taken aback. "I didn't realize your mother had died."

"She didn't. She left."

She bent to pick up a bright red leaf on the ground, twirled it around by the stem, and then let it fall back to where she'd picked it up from.

"Where did she go?"

"No one knows," she said. "Anyway, it doesn't really matter. We all move on, right? Thanks for coming across the street to help, but I guess I didn't need it."

"Did you find what you were looking for?"

"Yeah. And thanks for the cookies. It's nice to meet you."

"You're welcome," I said.

We stood there for a moment. I wondered what else I could say so I didn't have to leave.

"Are you sure everything is okay?" I asked.

"Why do you ask?" she responded, without turning around.

"You just look upset," I said, slowly following behind her.

"I'm okay."

"I don't mean to pry," I tried one more time, "but you really look like you're upset about something. And I hate to leave someone if I can help them."

She turned around to face me.

"I actually think the cookies are about the best thing you could have done. Russian teacakes are my favorite."

"I know they are traditionally a Christmas cookie, but I eat them year round."

"I haven't had them in a long time. My mom always made them for me the Sunday before Christmas. That was our Christmas cookie baking day."

I didn't say anything.

"So, thanks. I really appreciate it. It was...great timing."

"You're welcome," I said. "It was nice to meet you."

"Likewise. I'll tell my dad you stopped over."

"Okay."

"And don't be a stranger," she said. "Okay, Niles?"

I smiled the warmest smile possible and walked back to my house.

Be a stranger, Stefia? I wouldn't have dreamt of it.

**

A loud rap on my front door a week later sent the dog barking and my two cats hiding. I moved the curtain in the living room to peek out and see who was standing on the front step.

Stefia.

I kicked at the dog to shush him and he retreated to his bed near the stairwell. I tucked in my shirt, took a deep breath, and opened the door.

"Stefia!" I said, "What a nice surprise!"

"Hi, Niles. I just came over to return this platter you brought the cookies over on. Thanks, again."

I took the tray from her and grinned graciously. I caught her sneak a glance past me into the house

"Oh gosh," I said. "Don't mind the mess. It's just been crazy with the moving and…"

"Don't worry about it, Niles," she said. "You're in the middle of trying to fix up the house you just moved into. Besides, I would think you were a little weird if you kept everything totally spotless. Then you'd be like my mom. And that's not how real people live."

That girl. She was something else.

"Would you like to come in?" I asked. "I've just made some pumpkin bread."

She pulled her phone out of her back pocket, presumably to check the time. As if on cue, Magpie the dog, crept off his dog bed and snuck around the corner to us.

"Aww, you've got a dog!" Stefia said, her voice rising into a squeal. She put her phone back in her pocket and bent down to Magpie. He got excited, jumped, and licked at her face.

"Magpie, down!" I said, embarrassed that he was jumping all over her.

"It's okay, I love dogs. I wish I had one. What kind of dog is she?"

"She is a he," I corrected, "and he's a beagle."

"I love his ears!" she said, running her hand down the length of his long flaps. "How old is he?"

"Five," I answered. "But he thinks he's still a puppy."

Magpie stopped licking Stefia and ran to get his toy—a ratty old stuffed bunny— and dropped it by where she was knelt on the ground.

"You brought me a toy?" she said to Magpie. "You want me throw this, huh? Do you, boy?"

With Stefia and Magpie lost in a game of fetch, I went to the kitchen and sliced some of the warm pumpkin bread. I placed it, along with a stick of butter and a knife, on the same orange tray she had returned. It smelled absolutely delicious, even without its usual cream cheese icing. I left the kitchen carrying the tray and set it on the dining room table near the game of fetch.

"I brought out the pumpkin bread, just in case you wanted to try some," I said.

"Oh, okay," she said, as Magpie brought the bunny to her. He didn't drop it in her lap, though. He wanted to play tug.

"Give it up, Magpie!" she said to him, giggling and pulling at the bunny latched in his teeth. But Magpie didn't release his clenched jaw. Instead he tore away, bunny still intact, victory his, and went to his dog bed to chew the bunny's ear.

"I guess he was done," I said. "He's kind of the boss of the bunny."

Stefia smiled, stood, and came to the dining room table.

"The bread looks delicious," she complimented.

"Thanks. Have a seat. I mean...if you want."

She sat, folded her hands in front of her, and looked about the room.

"You seem to be quite the wizard in the kitchen," she said.

"Why do you say that?" I said, and offered her a slice of bread with half a slab of butter.

"Well," she said, taking the bread, "every time I've seen you, you've got delicious food."

"We've only seen each other twice," I reminded her. "It could be a coincidence."

"Not likely," she said, and shoved part of the bread in her mouth.

I took a bite of the bread, too, and was pleased that it tasted so good. The texture was soft and the flavor melted onto my tongue. It was rich and full and practically perfect.

"Mmmm. This is really good, Niles," she said. "You *are* a wizard in the kitchen."

"Thanks," I said. "Do you bake at all?"

"Nope. My middle sister, Naomi, is kind of the kitchen queen now that mom is gone."

She chewed the rest of her slice of bread in silence; I suppose that she was thinking on her middle sister or her mother or maybe even how to make pumpkin bread. Then I caught her looking at the pictures I had framed all around the antique buffet opposite my dining room table.

"Those are pictures from when I used to live in Virginia," I said.

"How long did you live there?"

"Most of my life," I said.

"What brought you here?"

"I surely don't know," I said with a chuckle. When she looked at me cockeyed, I said, "Who moves to Minnesota by choice?"

"What's wrong with Minnesota?"

"One word: Winter."

Stefia laughed.

"I've never lived anywhere else," she said. "Minnesota winter is normal to me."

"You're one tough cookie. Do you want another piece of bread?"

"Can I?"

"Absolutely."

"Okay," she said, and reached across the table for another slice. "I think this is the best pumpkin bread I've ever tasted."

"Thanks."

"But seriously," she said, swallowing. "Why Minnesota? There's forty-eight other states besides here and Virginia. Why choose somewhere whose only claim to fame is the longest winter ever?"

"Actually, that would be Alaska, I think," I said, and reached for a second piece of bread myself. "And to be honest, most of what I heard of Minnesota before moving here was about the greatness of the Mall of America, and that you have a pretty amazing theater circuit."

She swallowed the bread that was in her mouth and choked a bit. She cleared her throat and coughed to help it go down.

"Are you okay?" I asked, rising. "Do you need some water?"

She nodded and I brought her a full glass from the kitchen. She drank the whole thing and then smiled uncomfortably.

"Sorry," she said. "I guess I just swallowed wrong."

"Are you sure you're okay?"

She nodded.

"What were we talking about?" she asked. "Oh, yes. Minnesota stuff. I've never been to the Mall of America."

"Really? It's right here in your state and you've never been?"

"Nope. Way too big. I heard if you spent just ten minutes in every store or attraction at the mall, you'd be there for four days. And that's without even sleeping."

"You're not a shopper?"

"Nope. I know, weird for an almost 14 year old girl."

I practically choked on my bread. Was she kidding me?

"You're only thirteen?" I said.

"Yeah." She pushed the rest of the bread into her mouth and licked her fingers. "Well, I'll be fourteen in a couple weeks."

"Oh," I said, swallowing hard. I had to look away from her. I had looked at pictures, the butter knife, the yarn coming off the edge of the rug the dining room table was sitting on. I looked for anything to distract me from the fact she was at least five years younger than what I'd originally pegged her as.

"What is it?" she asked.

"Nothing."

"You thought I was older?"

"I did," I confessed.

"I get that a lot," she said, looking at the pictures again. "I had someone ask me where I was starting classes this year. I think they thought I was in college. I laughed and told them I was just starting high school."

"Could have fooled me," I said, my head spinning in any direction it could to change the subject.

"It's an honest mistake, Niles. Don't worry about it. I hear it a lot."

I had to change the subject.

"I don't think it's weird that you're not a shopper," I said. "In fact, it's kind of refreshing."

"I suppose you haven't had time to go to the mall yet..."

"Nope. I've only been here, what, three weeks? I'm still stuck wondering how to make it through one of your winters."

"You'll be fine," she said and giggled. "It will make you tough."

"Yeah, toughen me up, that's what I need," I said. "Anyhow. I chose Minnesota for a few reasons, but a big one was a friend of mine who actually doesn't live too far away. James Harper. We went to college together."

"James Harper? Never heard of him."

"Really? I thought everyone knew everyone in a small town."

"Is this a small town?"

"I think it is."

"Nah, a small town is Fletcher. They've only got a population of like, sixty people. That's a small town."

"That's not a small town...that's a family reunion."

Stefia giggled and shoved the last of her second piece of bread in her mouth.

"That seriously is the best bread I've ever tasted," she said. "Did you go to college for kitchen wizardry?"

"Nope, I just like to bake. I went to college for stage wizardry."

"Huh?"

"Theater. But not really the acting part. More the backstage stuff. Lights, set design, things like that. My friend that I mentioned, James Harper, he was there for acting."

"Was he good?"

"He liked what he did, and I think that was the important thing."

"So he wasn't good?"

"He had passion."

"Oh."

"That's kind of why I moved here, though. James is trying to start up this little community theater, kind of between here and St. Cloud? I'd been through some junk out in Virginia, life changes and all, and he tossed it out in the air that I should move here and help him start it up."

"I see."

"I think he kind of meant it as a joke at first. One of those jokes where you toss it out as an idea, not thinking anyone

84

will actually bite, but then they do, and you're glad they did?"

"Yeah."

"So, that's kind of what I'm involved in now. Getting the theater up and running."

She had suddenly grown quiet. She looked off out my front window towards her house. Towards that tree I saw her sitting by and searching underneath a week ago.

"Sorry," I said. "Here I am babbling along, telling you boring stories about old friends and silly dreams. Let's talk about you for a while."

She smiled. And for an almost fourteen-year-old, it seemed to be a smile that showed wisdom beyond her years.

But it also showed something else: ambition.

"I want to be an actress," she said, suddenly.

"Oh?" I said, surprised at the irony in her confession. What were the chances?

"Yes."

"You're interested in the theater?" I could hardly breathe, my heart was beating so fast. Stefia...an actress?

"I take that back," she said, seemingly involved in a conversation more with herself than with me. "I don't want to be an actress. I'm *going* to be an actress."

Her announcement changed everything. There was a conviction in her voice; a conveyance of eagerness. An unquenchable zeal. A ravenous appetite for something just out of reach. Something I could tell she would pull into herself and accomplish.

"You like to act?"

"I do. Doesn't everybody?"

"Only the crazy ones," I said with a smirk. "How many shows have you done?"

She looked straight at me and answered unapologetically.

"None."

"What?"

"None." Her serious, defiant eyes made me believe that it almost didn't matter. "But don't worry. The fact I've never been on stage makes no difference. I'm going to be an actress."

"There's an audition coming up in a month for the first play that the Crystal Plains Theater is putting on," I said, hardly believing my luck. "I could help you prepare an audition piece. I mean, if you wanted."

"Really? You could?"

"I've been around theater all my life. I could give you some pointers."

"Really?" Her voice turned upwards into a squeal that brought Magpie back over to her feet.

"Sure," I said. "Not a problem."

"Okay! When can we start?"

"How about in two days. I can start with helping you find a monologue."

"Sounds awesome," she said. "Thanks, Niles!"

"Anytime."

Stefia was so excited she bolted out of her chair, and went for the front door.

"This is gonna be great!" she said to Magpie. "I'm going to be an actress and people are going to come from miles around to see me perform."

"You think so?" I said.

"People are going to remember my name, Niles. I'm gonna prove it to you. People will not forget me."

And something about the manner in which she moved, the way the light soaked into her face, and how her rich voice wrapped around the words she spoke, made me believe what she had said. People wouldn't forget Stefia. Of that I was absolutely sure.

**

Two days later, Stefia was on my front step with a Kindle full of monologues, wanting me to help her choose which ones were best. I told her not to go with something the director would have heard a hundred times at every audition he held.

"Find something different. If do the same thing as everyone else, the director will assume you're like everyone else. And you're not."

"Okay."

"That goes for the audience, too. You have to give them something different, otherwise you just fade into their memory as being in a show that was just like every other show they have ever seen."

She looked through the monologue books and couldn't find anything she liked so I went through my stash and gave her a copy of a piece from *Patient A*.

"Try this," I said. "It's pretty deep. It will set you apart. And they will never guess you are only thirteen."

"I'm almost fourteen."

"Yeah," I said, tasting the saliva that had collected in my mouth.

She skimmed through the paper I'd handed her.

"What's it about?"

"A young woman who gets diagnosed with HIV."

"Oh god, really? Are you sure?"

"Yes. I'm sure."

So she started reading it. Her voice shook with nerves through the first paragraph.

The first time I was tested for HIV, the test wasn't conclusive. So I had another one. That was inconclusive, too. So I had one more. Five days after I turned twenty-two, the results came back positive. The doctor gave me some time alone, before my folks came in. I began to cry. I looked out the window, and the clouds were moving against the sun, swirling.

But the farther she read down the sheet I had handed her, the better she sounded.

My mother was the first to come in. She knew as soon as she looked at me. She came around and just lunged onto the bed and cried and hugged me and pushed my hair back and...comforted me. She talked about her own parents, who'd been killed years before in a car accident and how they'd be waiting in heaven for me, along with Grandma Zebleckas and even their dog that died, too. I think if she could have put everything that had ever lived into heaven for me at that moment, she would have.

By the time Stefia had reached the end of the monologue, I was completely captivated by her voice, her face, the way her mouth formed the words that others had written, the way she conveyed a meaning beyond what the author had known.

When we'd calmed down, my father came in. That was harder... He shook, and he cried... I said, "Put your head on my shoulder," and he did. And I... petted his head, and said, "It's going to be ok. We're going to get through this." And Mom was rubbing his back, and he just kept crying and crying. He kept saying it had to be a mistake, that he didn't believe it, that it can't be. It just can't be. And I said, "Dad, it is."

After a full ten seconds of silence and multiple deep breaths, she asked, "Well, how did I do?"

Oh. God.

How could I even attempt to describe how she'd done? Even if my throat wasn't completely dry I would not have even known the words to explain the passion, the intensity, the emotion. All from an almost fourteen-year-old girl.

She was a natural.

Oh. God.

"Really, really well," was all I could get out before I had to swallow.

And that was the understatement of the year. People always talked about actors who were naturals, people who were just born with the art in their blood. I had never believed it was possible. I figured talented actors took a ton of classes and honed their art through mentors who had done the same thing. Have a love for the craft? An interest in the art? Sure. But to be a complete stage virgin, cold read through a monologue...and totally nail it?

I'd found a diamond. I'd struck gold. And this girl was going to bring the Crystal Plains Theater to life.

"You should audition for the part of Candace in the upcoming show," I said, calmly.

"Why?"

"Because you look the part."

I handed her a copy of the script, and she thumbed through the first few pages scanning for Candace's lines.

"But...Niles, it says Candace is the lead female."

"Yes. You can handle it. I have faith in you."

"But...it says here that Candace is seventeen. I'm only thirteen."

"You'll be fourteen in a few days," I said. "And besides, people always mistake you for way older. Look, this is acting. It's all about appearances. It's all about what you can make people believe."

She pondered that, letting it swirl around in her brain and take on whatever meaning it needed to have for her.

"I can make people believe a whole lot," she finally said.

"Good. It will make things a whole lot easier."

**

She was so nervous. She was sweating buckets and her hands were shaky. I told her not to be so nervous, that she was wonderful at what she was doing and she'd practiced.

"But look at everyone else who is here!" she said.

"Don't worry about them. Focus on yourself."

It seemed weird to say something like that. It's counterintuitive to how we are brought up. Think of others. Think of how you can help. Think of how they might feel. But in the theater, it's different. It's cut throat. It's every man for himself. It's push yourself forward and say why you're the best person for the part.

It's drama.

Stefia was called up on stage for her audition. And while she weaved her tale, the director looked up. He set his pen down and relaxed in his seat and actually smiled. Then he looked at my friend, James Harper. And James looked at me.

And mom was rubbing his back and he just kept crying and crying.

He kept saying it had to be a mistake, that he didn't believe it, that it can't be.

It just can't be.

And I said, "Dad, it is."

The audition panel erupted into applause and I knew she had the part. She deserved it.

She stood on stage, surprised but soaking in their applause. I waved her off stage and she bolted down the side stairs and wrapped her almost fourteen-year-old arms around me.

Oh, God.

Don't.

I patted her back and smiled.

"Now what?" she said.

"Now you wait for a phone call or an email to tell you if you got a part."

"I think I will die waiting!"

"Anticipation is good," I said. "It makes the prize better."

**

Two days later, on her birthday, they called to offer her the part of Candace.

I heard her screams all the way over in my yard. She came flying out the front door of her house

"I got the part, Niles! I got the part! It's for real!" She jumped at me with a hug.

93

Please.

Don't.

Just stop…

I hugged her back.

"That's great!" I said. "Congratulations!"

"Oh my god, Niles," she said, excited and out of breath, "I'm a real artist now. A real artist!"

I couldn't wipe the smirk from my face. She thought she was the artist, but she was actually the art. Like a masterpiece forgotten in an attic that I'd stumbled upon at a yard sale and knew the world needed to see.

Now, let's be honest. Stefia would have gotten the part even on her own merits, but between you and I, the part of Candace had been secured for her. James Harper owed me a favor, and seeing Stefia play Candace in the show was something I wanted more than most things in my life.

Yes, James Harper had owed me a favor. And his granting of said favor opened a floodgate that changed Stefia's life forever.

And mine.

**

After the first run was done and the cast party had ended, I drove her home from the theater. As her commentary whirled around on the ecstasy of completing her first official role, I pulled my olive green classic Cutlass into my driveway and parked.

"Thanks for driving me home, Niles. You've been such a huge help to me. I don't know how I can ever thank you."

"It was worth every minute," I said. "Totally my pleasure to be of assistance."

She got out of the car and headed down the driveway to her house.

"Oh, hey," I called after her, like it had been an afterthought and not a plan. "Do you want to come in for a second? I have this new piece that I think you should take a look at."

"A new piece? For what?"

"Just come inside for a minute," I said. "Take a look at it. I think it will be perfect for your next audition."

She nodded and I unlocked the front door of my house.

"Make yourself comfortable," I said, motioning to my red leather couch. I went to get the scene that was still sitting in the printer. She sat down, checked her phone, and laughed as she returned a text.

"Someone sending you jokes?" I asked as I walked back into the room.

"No. Just another *you were so wonderful in the production* text. I still can't believe how awesome it all is."

"People love you. You're a natural."

She smiled.

"Now," I said, sitting down next to her and handing her a copy of the new scene, "this is a piece for two people. I know your last audition you only had to give a monologue, but there might be callbacks for this next show and you'll probably be asked to read against someone in a scene before they make their casting choices."

"Well, if I got called back…"

"Yeah. If."

I smiled at her and then looked down at the paper.

"Shall we?" I asked.

She nodded.

She read her part and as she concentrated on the lines, my hand crept across the cushion of the couch and rested on her thigh.

"Niles," she said, scanning her eyes quickly down the page. Her eyes fixed on my fingers spread out on her thigh. "That's not in the script."

"No. It's not."

"Niles, don't…"

I slid a finger up to my lips to shush her, and then pushed her back to lie down on the couch. Her eyes were fat with panic and her breath tangled somewhere inside her chest. I watched her head meet the cushion, her hair spill out all around her face, and her lips part to say something—but I never heard what it was. All I knew was that my hot breath on her face as my hands fumbled with the hem of her skirt was melting what little bit of girl was left inside her.

The look on her face.

Oh, god.

I will never forget that look.

**

At 6:30 am on a Sunday morning, two weeks after that first run ended, I sat at my dining room table drinking a mug of equal parts Baileys and coffee. The slow swirl of light into dark was mesmerizing and I resisted the urge to stir it all together with my spoon.

A quiet tap on the front door shook me and when I looked up to the etched pane of glass I'd just changed out three days earlier, I saw the outline of someone who looked a lot like Stefia.

I opened the door and neither of us said anything. I could hardly believe she was standing in front of me.

She'd come back.

"Hi," she squeaked after a minute.

"Hi."

It had snowed the night before and her boots made prints on the porch.

"Do you want to come in?" I asked. "It's cold..."

"No."

The knitted red mittens she wore looked warm, but she rubbed her hands together and blew on them even so.

"Look," she said, agitated and almost impatient. "Auditions are the beginning of next month."

I watched the squint of her eyes as she focused on a drip of paint that had dried on the spindle of the porch. She wouldn't even look at me.

"Niles, I need your help to audition."

"I'd be more than happy to..."

"Don't say anything," she said, looking to the ground and kicking her boot at the snow that had warmed to slush under her feet. "Just let me talk."

The cold air drifted into my house and I heard my furnace kick on. I didn't dare ask her a second time to come inside, so I stepped out on the porch and pulled the door closed behind me.

"I need to be on stage, Niles. I need this theater. I can't even explain it to you because it doesn't make any sense to me."

"You don't have to explain it to me, Stefia. I…"

"I shouldn't even be here talking to you. You get that, right? The last thing I should have done this morning was walk over here to talk to you. But I couldn't stop."

Stefia pulled her hat down further over her ears and then wrapped her arms around herself.

"I was ready to quit. I was going to just be done. I was going to…"

She looked at the railing of the porch, unable to finish. The cold had crisped the features of her face, pinching at her cheeks and eyes. Tears clung to the edge of her eyelids, but I knew it wasn't because she was crying.

"Theater is like a drug, darling," I said, breathing out a long sigh that looked like a string of smoke in the cold air. "It's addicting. Makes a person do all sorts of things they wouldn't normally do."

She finally looked at me. Our eyes connected, hers boring into mine with a mix with ferocity and hope.

"Wait," she asked. "Are we talking about me…or you?"

"We're both her slave," I said, ignoring the question. "Once you're a part of the theater, the lines between real life and life on stage start to blur."

"And that's okay?" she spit. "It's just suddenly okay that everything is a blurry confused mess?"

"It doesn't matter if it's okay," I said. "It's just the way it is."

**

And so our odd life of being together—but pretending we weren't—went on. The blurry confused mess that was *us* made perfect, beautiful sense.

I know it did. Because she told me it did.

In the end, our secret died with Stefia. I know she never told another living soul because she told me she wouldn't. And I believed every word she ever said.

She was always good at making people believe.

-Taylor Jean-

I actually missed the first call about the shooting. When it rang through, I was laying on a table in Spencer Grove, waiting to donate blood for the first time. Afterwards, the irony made me gag, because it was Stefia who had always told me I was wimp for not having donated the minute I turned eighteen.

The nurse swabbed iodine all over the vein and then checked her watch.

"This has to sit on your arm for thirty seconds," she explained, "and then you're ready to rock."

She unwrapped the needle and placed it next to where she was going to punch it under my skin and into my vein.

"If you think you're gonna be one of those people who don't like to watch," she said, "now would be the time to look away."

"Nah. I'm okay," I said. "I actually like to watch."

**

Stefia and I were the same age but since I was part of that underground, radical unschooling, hippy Christian world, we weren't in the same grade. I first knew Stefia from church. We became good friends at thirteen when we were old enough to join the choir. The older ladies called us the Giggle Girls because we were always chatting and laughing while the other sections practiced their parts. We'd talk about beads and bands and books we'd read and boys we thought were cute.

And we talked about coffee. My family owned the coffee shop in Granite Ledge and I got Stefia a job there as soon as she turned fifteen. I thought I would have to work pretty hard to convince my parents that Stefia would be a worthy addition to our list of employees, seeing as how she wasn't part of the underground we normally associated with. As it turned out, they thought it was a great idea. Actually, they were completely enamored with Stefia—like most adults seemed to be—and jumped at the opportunity to employ her. See, everyone thought Stefia was mature. And responsible. And had a pleasing personality.

To be honest, she was just about everything you could want in someone else.

Stefia had this voice that was syrupy and maple, a voice that stuck you to what she was saying or singing. It was like the cinnamon sugar I put on my warm buttered toast every morning. She was the perfect complement to everyone around her, a chameleon who could talk to anyone. And yet, as much as she seemed to be able to meld herself to any situation, she wasn't fake. Her interest in people was completely genuine.

And maybe that's why I clung so tightly to her as a friend. If I was with Stefia, maybe a little of what everyone wanted would rub off on me.

I could only hope.

I think that's why I liked to watch her. Probably why we all did. I mean, she was gorgeous. A kind of gorgeous that took her beyond trying to look like every other girl our age that followed some fad to be pretty. Stefia was her own breed of beautiful. She didn't even have to try. Watching her was the closest thing to being her that we'd ever get.

Stefia had this guy friend named Elliot who was always following her around. They weren't together or anything. He was more like a brother, she said. He was a year older than us; kind of cute and awfully nice, but his younger brothers were jerks. One of them, Mitch was his name, hated me for about a thousand unknown reasons. Probably because I was homeschooled. Or wore too many beaded bracelets. Or because I wouldn't date him. Who knows. But this one day Mitch and Elliot came into the coffee shop just about the time Stefia and I were done with work.

"Can I get an Americano?" Elliot asked Stefia. "And Mitch...he wants...Mitch, what do you want?"

Mitch was watching me wipe coffee grounds off the back counter.

"Hey, Taylor Jean!" he said, way too loudly, ignoring his brother's question.

"What?"

"Are you lezzing out over there?"

"Huh?"

I realized that while I'd been wiping coffee grounds off the counter and into the trash can, I'd been staring at Stefia the entire time. And he'd seen me. I rolled my eyes at him and went back to straightening the counter.

"Should I call you TJ?"

"What's that supposed to mean?" I asked.

"You know, TJ. Like a guy's name, so you can stare at Stefia all you want and no one will think anything about it?"

"Don't be an ass, Mitch," said Elliot.

Stefia had started making Elliot's Americano but left it at the machine.

"Yeah, Mitch," she said as she walked over to me. She spun me around, held my cheeks in both of her hands, and kissed me squarely on the lips.

Then she glared at Mitch.

"And don't be jealous," she said to him, and winked.

Stefia was always doing things like that. One minute she'd be quoting Shakespeare or rattling off stats from the New York Stock Exchange. The next minute, she'd pull out something totally random—like kissing her female co-worker—and knock everyone off their feet.

Being around Stefia was magical. It made me feel like I was worth something. I would stare at her and imagine that indescribable thing she had that everyone wanted oozing off of her and right onto me.

Actually, Stefia and I kind of had a thing about being watched. It was an inside joke that turned into a huge philosophical discussion. It was just after my sixteenth birthday and I had invited her over to my house after work to hang out, eat crappy food, and watch YouTube videos because I had faster internet. We tripped upon a video titled *How to Make Hair Dye with Ketchup* and discovered it was actually a ridiculously lewd journey through what the YouTuber wanted to do with each and every girl on his local softball team.

"That's a little far," I said, as I clicked on the flag below the video to report it. "I mean, who makes this stuff?"

"People with too much time on their hands," Stefia said, dismissively.

"It's disturbing." I closed my laptop and shoved it further back on my desk.

"Oh, come on, Taylor Jean," Stefia said, flopping back on my bed and flipping her feet up on a stack of pillows. "Everyone likes to watch."

"What is that supposed to mean?"

Stefia grabbed a handful of butter spindle pretzels and shoved three in her mouth at once. She chewed slowly, and I could tell she was carefully choosing her words.

"Why do guys go to strip clubs?" she asked. "Why do we watch talk shows where people freak out and fight with each other?"

"I don't think those two things are the same..."

"Why not? What makes them different?"

"For one," I said, rolling my eyes, "guys are desperate perverts. That's why they go to strip clubs."

"I don't think that's true," Stefia said. "Okay, some guys are desperate perverts..."

"Like Mitch?" I interrupted.

"Like Mitch," she agreed. "But I don't think that's why they watch. I think it's something deeper than that. Something that everyone has inside. I mean, why do people watch a play?"

"To be entertained."

"But what if it's not an entertaining play?"

"Then," I said, grabbing my own handful of pretzels, "the actors have failed. Let that be a warning to you!"

Stefia giggled and shoved her hand back in the pretzel bowl.

"No," she said. "What I'm saying is some plays are entertaining by nature. A love story, a story where the guy gets the girl, a story where everyone gets what they want in the end. But what about the stories that aren't like that? What about stories about death and destruction? Certainly those aren't entertaining..."

"Not in the normal sense, no," I agreed. "Let me ask you a question. Why do you act?"

"Huh?"

"You're up there on stage and people are watching you. And obviously you're not uncomfortable or you wouldn't be up there. So...why do you act? Why are you on stage?"

Stefia thought for a minute, twirling her last pretzel in the air like she was writing on my ceiling.

"Because now that I've started, I think I would die if I wasn't on stage."

"That's kind of dramatic," I said. "Fitting, coming from an actress."

She giggled and ate her last pretzel. She put her hand back in the bowl and frowned, signifying the bowl was finally empty. Then, in true I-don't-care-what-you-think style, she turned the bowl over and stuck it on her head, salt spilling into her hair.

"I guess I just like to give people something to see."

"You're a nut." I laughed and flipped my hand at the bowl to knock off her crown.

"But you're watching," Stefia said and laughed, catching the bowl to put it back on her head. "So which of us is really the nut?"

"Stefia, get real. It's kind of hard not to watch you," I said. "You're a natural performer."

"Indeed," she said, and leaned backwards to flip off the bed. But she misjudged the distance, and as she went over, rammed her feet right into the full length mirror that hung on the wall.

"Oh, crap!" she said. She jumped up and stared at the mirror that splintered into a million jagged pieces. "I'm sorry!"

"It's okay," I said. "No biggie. Cheap mirror."

She crouched to the floor and checked for the few slivers of glass that had fallen out. Her heel had made a perfect bull's eye in the middle the mirror, but luckily, most of the glass remained fractured inside the frame.

"Everything okay up there?" my dad called from down the hall.

"Yeah!" I yelled. "Stefia's just up here trying to ruin my luck by busting mirrors."

"Need any help?"

I opened my bedroom door and yelled down the hallway, "No. We're fine. Really."

He didn't answer so I closed the door. And when I turned back into the room, Stefia was still staring into the broken mirror.

"Stefia. I said it was fine. Don't worry about it. The mirror only cost like five bucks at…"

"Have you ever noticed how the cracks in the mirror mess up the reflection?" she asked.

"Um…yeah. That's generally what happens when the glass breaks."

"But, like…look. The cracks are all you can see."

I picked up two pillows that had fallen on my lilac carpet and tossed them up on the bed.

"Yeah? So? What are you getting at?"

She kept looking at the mirror, brushing her finger lightly over her broken reflection.

"It's not like that with people," she said.

"Like what?"

"You know, with the cracks. There's a lot of people walking around that are really cracked."

"Stefia, what in the world are you talking about?"

"Most of the time with people," she said, "you can see everything *but* the cracks."

I threw a pillow at her.

"Stop being weird," I said, brushing her off and pelting her with a second pillow. "You don't have to impress me with your deep wisdom, you know."

I handed her the pretzel bowl.

"What's this for?" she asked.

"Stick it back on your head. It's getting way too deep in here."

She smiled and flipped the bowl back over her hair. She stepped up on the bed, blew me a kiss, curtsied, and sat back down cross-legged right in the middle of my comforter.

"You're watching," she said, pointing a finger at me.

"Stefia," I said, grabbing a bag of chocolate and tearing it open, "shut up."

**

For some reason, the whole *why do people watch* or *oh look, you're watching* became a thing between us. We'd be working at the coffee shop and catch someone staring at the happenings of another table and we'd snort to each other they're watching and quietly hum the theme from *The Twilight Zone.*

Like, we had this regular customer named Heidi. She worked rotating shifts in labor and delivery at the hospital and sometimes stopped by for a pick-me-up before her shift started. One day she was sitting at her usual table in the corner, reading on her Kindle, and the only other customers in the shop—a teenaged couple—started sniping at each other. At first you could tell she was annoyed, because the nitpicking was distracting her from the book she was trying to enjoy. But the longer they argued, the less she looked at her Kindle and the more she looked at them. She just stared, totally sucked into what they were allowing others to overhear. Like it was a show she was watching. Like they were performing for her entertainment. She set her Kindle down and sucked off the straw from her to-go cup and only looked away from them when it seemed they might look at her.

We did a lot of people watching during our shifts, and what we usually noticed was that lots of people were watching other people. But it took us forever to figure out the why in why people watch.

And then there was the day of the crash in front of the coffee shop. It was the middle of the afternoon on a Friday and Old Man Rogers fell asleep driving his farm truck right down Main Street. He plowed into a little yellow VW Bug that had Marissa Jenkins and her twin toddlers inside. Right in front of our coffee shop.

A few customers stood up at their tables with their hands over their mouths muttering *Oh nos* and *Oh my Gods*. One mother held her young son and put her hand over his eyes so he wouldn't see the carnage, but she was looking herself. Two customers ran up to the full glass panels of our store front and gaped at the gathering crowd. I ran but stopped when my hand hit the front door. I wondered if I should go out. I wondered what I would do. I wondered if I could do anything at all.

Stefia, of course, ran out and jumped into the middle of everything like it was part of a play that she'd been perfectly blocked for what to do. I mean, she was out there a full three minutes before the cops and firemen showed up.

Old Man Rogers was all bloodied, his face smashed into his steering wheel, head snapped at some odd angle. I couldn't even see Marissa in the puckered mess left of her little car. I noticed one of her kids in the back seat, motionless and staring blankly; the other had flown from the car and landed on the tar just two feet from one of the tables on our sidewalk. I knew neither one of them was still breathing.

The shriek of the sirens announced the emergency vehicles were just making the corner. The sirens wailed and screeched, growing louder as they sped closer. It was so strange to me that the louder the sirens got, the quieter the air around us became. Except for Stefia, we all just stood there, suspended in time, rooted to the tile or sidewalk we were standing on.

And all I could think was *We're watching. We're watching and we can't look away.*

**

It was hard to talk about watching after that. It was hard to even talk to Stefia after that. I suppose it was a mixture of disgust and guilt and anger and disbelief. I kept avoiding Stefia because I didn't want our "thing" to come up. But two weeks later as we sat in the choir loft and waited to sing for service, she passed a slip of paper down to me. It made its way across the music folders of Jeanie and Thomas and Albert and finally over to me.

"This better be good," Albert whispered, shooting a look that conveyed just how inappropriate it was to pass notes during the sermon.

I opened it up.

Taylor Jean,

I know now why people watch.

Stefia

After church, when we'd put our music away and descended from the choir loft, I pulled Stefia into a corner by the church office.

"What do you mean?" I hissed. "What's this note supposed to mean?"

She didn't say anything, just walked out the front door of the church with a look like I should follow her. So I did. All the way across the street to Beidermann's Ice Cream Shop. She ordered two salted caramel sundaes with pretzel topping, carried them outside to a table, and sat down.

"Here," she said, handing one to me. "I know you like pretzels so I ordered extra topping."

I sat down and took the sundae from her. After a minute of silence, in which I wondered what she was trying to do, I finally spooned a glob into my mouth.

"What's wrong?" Stefia finally said. "Why are things so weird between us now?"

I didn't say anything. Mostly because I didn't have an answer to her question. I didn't know why things were weird. They shouldn't have been.

"So, here's what I figured out," Stefia said, like someone had cut the scene we were in and started a whole new one. "I was thinking about our thing. You know, why people watch? And ever since that accident, I've been stuck on figuring it out."

"Stefia," I started, but she cut me off.

"No, it's fine. I think sometimes we learn the most in uncomfortable situations. And that was definitely uncomfortable."

"You were uncomfortable?" I said, incredulously. "You? Stefia, you jumped in there like you knew exactly what to do! The rest of us just stood there like complete dumbasses, just...watching."

And at watching, I lost it. I stabbed my spoon back in my sundae, set it on the table, and sobbed into my hands.

"Taylor Jean, stop," Stefia said. "Don't beat yourself up. Besides, it only *looked* like I knew what I was doing."

115

"Well, you're pretty damn good at looking like you know what you're doing."

Stefia took a bite of her sundae, putting the spoon in her mouth upside down and sucking the ice cream off the back of it.

"I've been told that before," she said.

I rubbed beneath my eyes with the tops of my pointer fingers and said, "I'm such a baby. I bet I look stupid."

"Nah," she said, and then added with a smirk, "do you believe me?"

I smacked her on the shoulder.

A chickadee sat in the branch above our table, sputtering out his call. I looked up into the leaves and wondered what it would be like to wing around over everything, watching people live their ridiculous lives. Had the chickadee been at the accident? Had he flown over Marissa's car moments before Old Man Jenkins rammed its engine into the backseat?

"So what did you figure out?" I asked. "I mean, about why people watch?"

"Oh," she said. "That. Well, like I said, after the accident I really started thinking about this whole thing. Why were people standing around watching? I mean, it wasn't pretty at all. I think the top half of Marissa's body was thrown about fifty feet from her car."

"Yeah," I said, shaking the memory from my head. "I know."

"And I guess what I decided was that people watch so they can be involved without really being involved. They can part of something. They can say they were there, but at a safe distance."

"Wait a second. I did not keep watching because I wanted to be a part of the carnage," I told Stefia. "You're wrong."

"Don't you get it?" she asked. "It was okay for you to watch. Everyone was watching and no one was judging anyone for watching. I mean, think about it. You can witness something like that, something you don't normally see every day. You're drawn to it. You're part of the experience. You don't have to look away. Everyone is gawking so it's okay if you do it, too."

"I wanted to help, Stefia. I wanted to jump in there, but I just couldn't..."

"And that, Taylor Jean, is why you watched. You could have looked away, you could have ignored it, but you didn't. You watched."

I watched.

**

I'm still wearing the Band-aid over where the nurse plunged that needle under my skin a month ago to suck out my blood. It's a multicolored Band-aid that says "Give" and it doesn't match at all with the dress I'm wearing to the funeral.

And I really don't care. Because right now I'm stuck on thinking about the things we see, and what we watch, and how it tells a lot about us when it's all said and done. I'm choking on the bitter realization that in the end, the Stefia that everyone got to see was not the beautifully perfect, warm maple syrupy Stefia that they wanted, but instead a broken Stefia fallen in the middle of five of her fellow actors in a puddle of blood and piss.

Not exactly what the audience paid to see.

But, then, everybody likes to watch.

-Kristopher-

If people were honest, they'd all admit to being like an iPod left on shuffle. No one's song fits in any single file.

"Why is that, Kristopher? Why do you say that?" she had asked me that night.

"Because we are all different people with every person we know," I answered.

"How do we know then who anyone really is?"

"I guess we don't. No...I know we don't.

My dad, James Harper, started up the little Crystal Plains Theater about four years ago with his old college buddy, Niles. My parents were wannabe actors with old money; Niles was a stage wizard with a penchant for collecting odd things. The three of them imagined that our little town needed some culture and figured community theater was the way to put Granite Ledge on the map. At first, everyone laughed. They said *this isn't New York* and *what's wrong with the plays at the elementary school?*

Stefia changed all that. No one would admit it, but I think she was a big reason people came to the theater. The other actors were good, but Stefia...holy shit. She seriously belonged somewhere else—like New York.

I mean, just to watch her on stage? Holy shit. You know how someone walks in and you just know they've got it? That was her. My dad said so, Niles said so, the directors said so, and the audience said so—over and over again. It's like the mighty gods of theater dropped her in this little town as an itty bitty present for all of us to unwrap and enjoy.

Merry freaking Christmas. And Happy Hanukah, too.

My mom and dad were all about theater. They were crazy hyper, in your face extroverts who aspired to be awesome actors but never quite got there. Because you know, you can either act or you can't. That's just the way it is. But they had passion—and money—so they opened a theater instead. How they ended up with an introverted, mandolin playing son is beyond me. They always pushed at me to bust out of my shell and pop up on stage with everyone else. But there were only, like, four people in the world who were ever allowed to hear me play.

Stefia made five.

I had watched Stefia from the audience since the first show she was in, way back when she was fourteen and I was just old enough to drive myself to the theater to watch her. I never talked to her. I made it a point not to talk to her. It was easier to keep my fantasy alive that way. It was easier to pretend the reason we never talked was because there was no time, not because she wouldn't give the time of day if there ever was.

I'm not stupid. Stefia could have anyone. So why would she have me?

"How do we know then who anyone really is?" she had asked that night.

We don't, Stefia. We can't.

**

I waited for her that night.

I'd tossed dad some line about hanging out late at the theater to see if I could imagine myself on stage. He nodded, and then sighed like I'd finally seen the light.

"Make sure you lock up when you leave," he called after me as I walked out the door with my mandolin.

She's a beautiful instrument; a specially ordered red Gibson F-style mandolin. A ridiculous price tag, but I guess that's the perk of having parents with money. Or should I say, parents who want to see you on stage and happen to have money to blow.

At the theater, I sat in the unlit house as the actors milled around on stage, collecting their things after rehearsal. Although I wasn't a fan of being on stage, I enjoyed sitting in the audience. The cushion of the seat, the anticipatory silence, the crisp air, the way each person enjoyed a different performance of the same show depending on what seat they chose and where their mind traveled to when they sat down.

I knew Stefia hadn't left yet. She was in the wings, stage left, talking to Niles. Niles often came to the theater just to check up on things. Neither he nor my parents ever really helped out with much—directing, stage stuff, or casting— but I guess when you're part owner you like to hang out and see what's what.

After a minute, Niles walked down the steps to the right of the stage and out the exit door into the parking lot. From my estimation, that left Stefia and I as the only people in the theater.

From a lit stage, it's hard to see past the second row of the audience. I was sitting in the 14th so I stayed well concealed. Well, that was until I started playing my mandolin.

I don't mind saying that I'm good at playing. I wasn't good at much—I'd barely graduated two years earlier and I was never popular because I didn't care for sports—but music,

I was good at music. I was good at the mandolin— as good as Stefia was on stage.

The kicker, and the entire reason I was sitting in the audience playing, was that I happened to know that Stefia liked the mandolin. A lot.

How did I know that? An introvert listens. An introvert observes. And an introverted quiet mandolin player will sit in wait until the skills he has can win him something he wants.

It didn't take long until Stefia appeared around the corner of the curtain, craning her neck to see where the music was coming from. She shaded her eyes from the stage light that, for some reason, was still on, trying to see if she could identify who was playing the music. She closed her eyes, swayed her head with the classical tune I delivered, and lilted around the stage. When I finished the song, she clapped her hands.

And I wished those hands were around me. I wished she would take those hands and...

"You're good," she said in my direction.

I didn't say anything.

"God...like, really good. Have you been playing long?"

"Awhile."

"Do I know you?"

"No."

She left open a silence just long enough for me to slip into another song. I didn't think about the notes. I have never had to think about the notes. It left me free to study her face while she listened to me play. My fingers frisked along the length of the strings, her lips spreading into a smile that seemed too big for her face. She punctuated the end of my song with a well placed sigh.

"I absolutely love the mandolin," she said, opening her eyes. "You're very talented."

"I've heard the same about you."

"Do I know you?" she asked again.

I didn't answer.

She walked to the stairs off the side of the stage.

"Stay on the stage," I said. "Or I'll stop playing."

She grinned like we were playing a game.

"Why are you here?" she asked. "I mean, do you have a reason to be here? Are you picking someone up? Because I don't think there is anyone left to..."

"I'm waiting for someone. I thought I'd sit and play while I waited."

"But there's no one else here..."

"You're here, aren't you?"

She didn't respond although I could tell she wanted to. She wanted to know who I was; she wanted to know how I knew who she was. It was right there on the tip of her tongue. But hearing the music that I refused to stop playing was mind-numbing, and she had no problem giving herself over to its power.

See, people who don't understand music can't possibly conceive that it's the same as a drug. It can screw with your mind. It can give you power. It can weaken you. It can take over your head—both playing it and hearing it. Know how you're driving and you hear a song on the radio you like and you look down and you're going eighty miles an hour? That's the music speaking to you. Music gives you power. Music inspires. Music can take away your troubles...or give you everything you want. I guess it was all in how you looked at it.

**

My hands had never been clumsy. My fingers were always nimble and quick like Jack. But somehow when I pushed her against the door of the orchestra pit, one palm pressing into her hip bone, the heel of my other hand under her jaw, my hands felt thick and stupid. For half a second, I wasn't so sure of what I was doing anymore.

Fuck. Help me. I need to finish this.

She felt small in my hands. When I pushed my open hand from her hip up along her ribcage, spanning my fingers to take her all in, I was stupefied at how minuscule she suddenly felt. This girl I'd watched for four years, who had tangled herself into every corner of my brain, who commanded respect from her peers and applause from her audience, now felt little. Inconsequential. How could that be?

My lips brushed at her neck and I pulled in the smell of her; the mix of a nameless flowery perfume and sweat from a two hour rehearsal. She was there, right in front of me. I was inhaling her. I was tasting her. It was real.

My thumb wrenched into her ribs right under her breast and my other hand was wrapped behind her neck. I would take her. I would take her and everything that was in her.

But something didn't feel right.

She wasn't fighting. She acted like she should fight, but she didn't fight. And something about that was surprising enough…weird enough…wrong enough…that it caught me off guard and I found myself watching her eyes.

I mean, really watching. Searching for something. And I found it.

Something that was wrong.

Her transparent eyes brimmed with a sentiment I'd never been able to see from the audience. A disturbance you'd only notice if you got in close to her. If she let you in.

Fear.

I don't know how exactly I could tell, but I knew the fear wasn't directed at me. I sensed a fear like I'd stepped into a nightmare that was all hers and had nothing to do with me. Her eyes were full of something raw and desperate and somehow even though she was still fully clothed, she was more exposed than I'd ever imagined seeing her. And just for one second, I stopped. I stopped pushing and just held on.

"Help me," she whispered. And the inflection in her voice told me it was not a suggestion, it was a pleading and desperate solicitation.

"What?" I asked. "Help you?"

"Help me, Kristopher. Please."

Fuck. She said my name. She said my fucking name.

"You know who I am?" I clamored, my voice cracking with disbelief.

"Kristopher, please…"

"Wait. How do you fucking know who I am?"

My hands fell off of her, shaking. This changed everything.

"Just...help me," she breathed and blinked away a single tear.

"What do you want me to do?"

And I didn't have the first clue what was going to tumble out of her mouth. Reasons filled my mind—she needed me to take care of some asshole for her, she needed money, she wanted out of some mess at home. Fuck, why was she confiding in me? I came here to...

"Kristopher."

"What?"

"Finish what you came here to do."

I questioned her by staring just a half second too long and she answered by moving my left hand to where she thought it belonged.

The button of her jeans.

All at once, I didn't know what was happening. It was like she became my music. My skinny, long fingers danced across and inside her as if she was somehow predictable like the frets of my mandolin, which she wasn't...but somehow I knew what to do. I pressed and plucked and strummed and she sang like something amazing and beautiful and rare and impossible to recreate.

It wasn't the same anymore. It wasn't me going to the theater to do what I had planned to do. This was something entirely different. I wasn't forcing anything. I wasn't getting away with something I'd thought about every day since I'd first seen her. So what was I supposed to call it now? Unexpected, for one. Unexplainable, for two. Amazing and holy and screwed up and one hell of a mind game, for the rest.

Stefia was hurting. And she wanted me to take it away.

Of all people, me.

**

She stared up into the flies where the scenery hung, dragging her fingers across her bare stomach. She'd never been as beautiful as she was then; somehow broken, exposed, and turning me into a mystified mess. I got the feeling I'd touched upon something of hers that no one yet had, and I didn't mean any specific part of her body. No, it was deeper than that. Something she kept well hidden.

Stefia was an amazing actress.

"Play a song for me," she said, and then added, "Please."

As if I wouldn't have done it anyway if she'd demanded it like a snotty nosed two-year-old. As if I wouldn't help her in any way I possibly could.

My fingers danced across the instrument, hopping from one fret to another, jumping strings and making them ring out in ways that people would never imagine they could.

She continued her gaze into the flies of the theater, lost in thought, millions of miles beyond the roof of the building we were in. Off in the stars. Off to the things that shone almost as brightly as she did.

"Lost in thought?" I asked. I didn't know if I should even ruin the moment with the noise of my voice because sometimes words can be so ugly.

"Not really lost," she answered. "Just trying to figure out what I want."

"Sometimes that's hard to do."

"No," she corrected. "It's not hard to *know* what you want. It's hard to *get* what you want."

The irony of her statement almost made me laugh, since what I wanted basically opened itself up in front of me and begged.

"What is it that you want, Stefia?"

"I want someone to hold me and mean it. I want someone to talk to me because I'm me, not because I'm Stefia."

The way she said it made me cringe. The simplicity of her words up against the complexity of what they meant disturbed me and I stopped playing mid-song.

"Don't stop playing. Please."

"You don't have to say please," I smirked.

"Yes, I do," she said, with more weight in her words than seemed necessary. "I'm not special. I don't deserve special privileges."

"But you are special," I said, setting my mandolin down. "Don't you get that? You are so goddamn amazing, Stefia. You..."

"Don't."

"Why?"

"Just...don't."

And there was that look again. That fear. That heavy burden of something bigger than she could explain with words but couldn't hide if you got close enough to really stare into her eyes.

I wondered how many people had gotten that close.

"Let's not talk about it anymore," she said, sitting up and zipping her hoodie. "It's not worth arguing over."

"Were we arguing?"

She didn't answer.

"Can I ask a question?" I said.

"Sure."

"How did you know who I was?"

Stefia smiled.

"Why wouldn't I?" she said. "Your parents own the theater."

"But I'm never around. I've stayed hidden."

She paused before speaking, allowing a thoughtful smirk to dance across her lips.

"One can see a lot from up on stage," she said.

"But I've made it a point to hide."

"Sometimes we think we're hiding," she said. "Those can be the times we are most exposed."

A yawn finally escaped from Stefia's tiny perfect mouth. I checked my phone. 2 am.

"Time to shut this party down?" I asked. "Don't want your chariot to turn into a pumpkin."

"I'm no Cinderella, Kristopher."

I opened the stage door and let the both of us into the crisp fall air.

"Thanks for playing for me," she said. I was surprised that in all the events of the last three hours, she chose to talk about the music.

"You're welcome," I said. "Anytime."

"You mean that?"

"I do."

I didn't know if I should kiss her. I didn't know if I should open her car door or follow her home or what. I still didn't understand exactly what had happened or where any of it had left us.

"Kristopher?" she asked.

"Yeah?"

"Let's not tell anyone about this."

"Oh."

I tried to hide it. I tried to hide that I'd hoped she would say we could just vanish together. Or that I could be the person she chose to walk next to her; the one who everyone else knew was her protector. The person to breathe her in every night and lift her up every morning. I tried to hide it but there was just enough pain that eked through in my pathetic *oh*. And she heard it.

Shit.

"Shit," she said, at almost the same time I muttered it under my breath. "Kristopher. I don't…"

"No, it's okay."

"I mean, I'm not sorry it happened. Don't worry about the…"

"Okay."

"It's just that…"

"You don't have to explain it, Stefia," I said. "I get it."

"You do?"

"Yeah."

"Really?" She laughed. "Because you know what?"

"What?"

"I don't. I don't get it. And I couldn't explain it if I tried."

She leaned her back against her driver's side door and looked like she was going to cry. Real tears. Right there, in front of me.

"Shit, Kristopher, I hate this. I don't want to have to fucking worry about what anything looks like. I'm sick to death of worrying what people think and who will say what and how it will affect things that shouldn't even matter."

I wanted to throw up. My guts were turning and my throat was tight and I had to close my eyes because seeing her lash out made my insides come unglued. Watching her was like seeing a crystal ball shatter against a brick ledge.

"Stefia, it's okay. It's…"

"It's not okay, Kristopher. Stop saying that."

She put her head down and started shaking—little tremors that swelled and surged—and when she finally took a breath I could tell from the catch in her inhale that she was crying. Real crying, not blocked out stage crying. I didn't know this side of Stefia existed. I mean, she was Stefia. Solid and sure.

I couldn't stand it anymore. I hadn't understood anything about the night so far; I didn't know if I ever would. How was it that I'd shown up with the intention of taking everything I wanted, and ended up ripped apart because I realized she was hurting? I don't know why I cared. And maybe I should have, but I did.

Life is a funny thing.

I slid up to her, wrapped my arms around her shoulders, and pulled her into me. My long fingers weaved through her hair. I held her. I just held her and thought about how life twists and changes more than it stays the same and yet it catches us off guard every time.

"Just once," she said, "I want to be the one who writes the script."

I didn't answer.

"I'm tired of reading the lines other people make up, Kristopher."

I knew she wasn't talking about the theater.

If she could have melted into my chest, if I could have tugged her into my being, if I could have wrapped her up and pulled her into my heart I know I could have kept her safe from all the hurt she was feeling. And standing there with her head fit into the curve under my chin, her soft hair like a safe cushion for my thoughts, I felt like I could.

But I forgot that every now and again, things have a way of happening unexpectedly. And therefore, I completely failed at protecting her from the one thing she needed protection from.

Herself.

-Anna Marie-

I miss drinking coffee from a ceramic cup. For most of the past one hundred and seventy-two days, I've drank coffee from Styrofoam. I'm not supposed to have a ceramic mug in my room because they are afraid I will drop it. I'll admit I threw a bit of a temper tantrum and then Rowena, my nurse, she showed me right where they had written in The Policy that residents are not allowed to have ceramic cups in their room.

I don't like the coffee here. By the time it gets to my room it's lukewarm and my hazelnut powdered creamer doesn't mix right. I said to Rowena why can't you bring me hot coffee? Rowena said something back about The Policy and me dropping my Styrofoam cup and burning myself.

I've been drinking coffee longer than Rowena has been alive. I told her that. She just smiled and left for the next resident's room.

I'm a resident now.

The four walls of my room are pink. The first time Stefia came to visit she said the room reminded her of a bottle of Pepto-Bismol. I told her the first time I ever drank Pepto-Bismol I threw up. She giggled at that, and I knew we'd get along fine.

**

I didn't know why Stefia came to visit me. She wasn't family. I hadn't known her before I became a resident. All I knew about her was she acted at the Crystal Plains, she worked at the coffee shop in town, and she visited me once a week on Wednesdays. Sometimes you don't need to know everything about someone to talk about everything with them.

And oh, did we talk. About *everything*.

"I've got this situation with a guy," Stefia said the third time we met, "and I'm kind of wondering what to do about it."

"Stefia, dear," I said, sighing. "Have you ever raised goats?"

"No. What does that have to do with a guy?"

"Everything," I said and laughed. "Stay away from goats. And guys. Then you'll be fine."

One of the best things about Stefia's visits was she always brought a thermos of hot coffee and a blue and green striped ceramic mug for me to drink it out of. The fourth time she came to visit, Stefia stuck a small cardboard box in my closet and told me that was where I was supposed to hide my ceramic coffee mug when I was done using it.

"You're a rebel," I said with a giggle. "Why do you bring me coffee anyway?"

"Because I work at the coffee shop and I know coffee," she said. "And you deserve coffee that's warmer than piss."

That made me laugh.

Stefia served me the best cup of coffee every Wednesday. We laughed a lot on Wednesdays, which is good because as a resident you don't always laugh a lot.

Being a resident wasn't all it had been cracked up to be. I had family that visited occasionally. Bill and his wife, John and his kids, Diana and her daughter when they come home for holidays. James and Mary only dropped by when they didn't have some fancy thespian event to attend. When I was first put in the pink room, my family would visit all the time. But the longer I stayed, the less often they came. I could see the change in people. I'm resident and I won't ever *not* be a resident. They know this is where I will spend my end days.

These are my end days.

You could tell it in change of the way they talked to me. It was all together different. Like I was a two-year-old instead of their eighty-three-year-old mother. Grandmother. Great-grandmother.

I'm still here. Don't you see me?

I have lived a full life of a million things and yet they treat me like I don't know anything. They turn their voices up into cute phrases and talk louder than they need to. They want to talk about the football game we just watched or someone's cookies we just ate or who came to visit me yesterday as if my memory doesn't go back any further than twenty-four hours ago. It's the same for every resident here. I'm desperate to tell you about my life. I'm desperate to talk about the things that have mattered to me. None of the women in here are sweet little old women who knit to pass the time. That's just what we look like to you because that's what you want to see.

I am not the me that you see.

I was a painter, you know. No, you probably didn't know that. No one did. Because I painted pictures of flowers and horses and mountains I'd never seen while the kids were at school and then I burned the canvases so no one would know. And I wrote poems. I would stand at the sink doing dishes while Helmer was out doing who knows what and the kids were running through the house chasing each other. I wrote a lot of poems.

Stefia said I could still paint now. When I confessed to her that I used to paint, she asked why I stopped and I said because no one ever knew I started.

She said I might have been the next Picasso.

I told her there was no point in talking about regrets once you're a resident. Because at that point you can't do a thing about what you haven't done. And besides, everyone just wants me to sit in the corner and knit, anyway.

My grandson plays bluegrass. He's an absolute genius on the mandolin. I like bluegrass. Even the new progressive stuff. He once played me his favorite song; deep and pretty and something about how to grow a woman. Then there was this one line that talked about old folks in a home and *even though you love them you can't wait for them to go.* He stopped playing and apologized when he got to that part.

"Oh, shit, Grandma. I'm sorry, I didn't mean…" he had said.

"No worries, child," I had responded. "I get it."

"You do?"

I nodded.

I told him not to worry his head and to just keep playing. I know my family loves me, but now I'm just a resident. That's the way it is. You can't change the way it is.

You can lie about it, but you can't change it.

141

On the eighth Wednesday that Stefia came, I asked her why she came to visit me every Wednesday. She had never made me feel like a pity project, and as far as I knew no one had bribed her to come chat with me. I was the only one of forty-three residents with a predictable visitor every Wednesday at 3 pm.

"Aw, now Anna Marie, you know why I come here!"

"Nope, I don't."

"I heard there was someone here they were serving piss-warm coffee to, and I knew that just wouldn't do!"

"They are serving piss-warm coffee to everyone here, Stefia," I said as I laughed.

She laughed along with me, then after the giggles had subsided, she said, "Anna Marie, you're the only one who will tell it to me straight."

"What do you mean?"

"You tell me what you know. You don't lie. You don't hide," she said. "You don't act."

I thought for a minute and said, "Come close. I'm going to tell you the two absolute sure things I've learned from life."

"Okay, I'm ready." She leaned in to glean from me the wisdom I'd gathered in my eighty-three years on earth.

"Number one," I said, "you will never ever use Algebra in real life. Ever. And number two? There is no way for you to stop your dishrags from getting stinky. Just throw the damn things away and buy new ones."

Stefia opened up into a laugh that I didn't think could come out of that petite body of hers. She laughed so hard that she went silent and her body bounced up and down as she held her stomach and said, "Stop, oh my god, stop!" Her laughing got me laughing and I had to take off my glasses and I could hardly breathe. I thought I was going to have to call for oxygen.

After we'd recovered, Stefia poured another cup of coffee for the both of us.

"You must have one hell of a thermos there," I said.

"It's biggish."

"It keeps the coffee hot!" I said. "Maybe the home should invest in those."

A silence settled in while we sipped at our coffee. And it wasn't an uncomfortable silence, because pauses in conversation with Stefia never felt uncomfortable and the conversation never felt forced. But after some time had passed I spoke up.

"I have another story to tell you," I said.

"Okay."

So I began.

"Once upon a time there was a lady. She lived on a gravel road out in the middle of farm country. She was married and had a few kids. She had a country neighbor friend named Julie."

"Country neighbor?" Stefia interrupted.

"That means you're neighbors, but the houses out in the country aren't as close together as in the city. So someone can be your country neighbor and live a mile away."

"Oh," Stefia nodded. "Okay."

"So," I continued, "this lady had a country neighbor friend named Julie. Her kids and Julie's kids grew up together, hung out together, played and fought together. You know, like good friends do."

Stefia relaxed into her chair and sipped on her coffee listening to the tale as I wove it.

"Anyhow," I said. "So even though Julie's family and this lady's family were always together, there was something that just didn't seem right about how Julie's husband acted towards this lady. He seemed really stand offish. Really...stuck up. Really...I don't know, distant. Unreachable."

"What was the husband's name?"

"Which husband?" I asked.

"Julie's husband," Stefia clarified.

"Oh. His name was Grant."

"Okay," Stefia said. "Hey, Anna Marie?"

"Yeah?"

"You can just use your real name instead of 'the lady'. It makes it easier to follow."

I smiled.

"Can't get nothing past you, can I?"

"I didn't think you were actually trying to."

"I wasn't." I winked and took a sip of coffee. "Anyhow, so every time I'd be at Julie's farm visiting with the kids, Grant always had something to do. If I walked in, he walked out. If he was in the middle of something and I showed up, he disappeared. Drove me absolutely insane."

"I don't blame you," Stefia said.

"So one day after church, we were having a meal at Julie's farm. Dinner was ready so she sends the kids out to tell Grant it's time to eat. Well, the kids get sidetracked with something like kids always do. Julie's hands were full putting the last touches on a pumpkin pie so she asked me to go out to the machine shed and deliver the message to Grant myself."

I remembered that day like it was only an hour ago. I wandered out to the shed and found him tinkering with the tractor. I stood in the doorway, still in my flowery Sunday dress. He held up his hand to shield his eyes from the sun coming in the doorway so he could see who was watching him. When he realized it was me, he went right back to working on that tractor.

"Julie sent me to tell you dinner is ready," I said.

"Why didn't she send the kids?" No emotion. No *hi, how are you*. Nothing.

"She did. They got sidetracked."

He didn't say anything. Just messed with that tractor like I wasn't even there. And that's what he always did. Pretended I wasn't there. So I got mad. I snapped.

"What is your problem?" I snapped from where I stood in the doorway.

He glanced up at me but made no effort to stop what he was doing.

"Excuse me?"

"You have a problem with me?"

"What do you mean?"

He was trying to spin a wrench on a bolt and not having any luck. He kept forcing it, twisting and turning and

146

gritting his teeth and I started to wonder if the discomfort on his face had nothing to do with the bolt that wouldn't come off.

"Every time I come here, you walk away. Every time I enter the room, you leave. What on god's green earth did I do to make you not like me?" I yelled. "What the hell do you have against me?"

He gave one final jerk on the wrench. It flung the wrong way off the tractor, and he busted his knuckles against the stuck bolt. He sucked in his breath, shook out his hand, and then cradled it close to his body. Looking right at me over the top of the tractor with gritted teeth and fixed eyes, he finally entered into real conversation, carrying an intensity I'll never forget.

"You don't get it, do you?" he asked.

"Get what?"

"I can't be around you."

"Says who?"

He shook his head.

"I refuse to be around you."

"Why, Grant? Why do you hate me so much?"

"You don't get it!" he hissed. "I don't hate you!"

"Then what's the problem? Why can't you be in the same room with me?"

"I just can't."

"That's not a reason," I said. "Tell me why!"

"Because, Anna Marie!" he screamed. "Because! Okay?"

"No. I want to know. I want to..."

"I'm married," he said.

"What does that have to do with anything? You have to walk out of a room I'm in because you're married? Grant...I'm married, too! What does that..."

"Christ, Anna Marie. Your pretty head can't be that thick,"

"I'm not thick, Grant. " I said. "I just want you to come out and explain yourself. I want you to say it!"

He closed his eyes and balled up his fists. He shook his head, and then he kicked a tool clear across the floor of the machine shed.

"God damn it, Anna Marie! I can't be around you because I'm afraid of what will happen if I am!"

The words exploded with such a force that I knew closing his mouth around them wouldn't have stopped them from coming out.

"Grant?"

"Damn it," he said, his eyes fixed on me. "Just go."

I stared at him, consumed for what seemed to be an eternity. And then another one. And it wasn't until I heard the kids in the yard barreling towards the machine shed that our eyes broke their hold. It was then I remembered his knuckles, dripping spots of blood on the tractor.

"Do you want me to…" I started, motioning towards his hand, but he shook his head and grabbed a rag to wrap it up in.

"Just go," he said.

"But…"

"I meant what I said. I need you to leave."

"Grant?"

"Please. Just go."

So I did. I walked out of the machine shed and back to the house, each step away from him feeling like a knife through my heel.

"Did he ever come in for dinner?" Stefia asked, breaking into my thoughts and momentarily forcing me back to present day. She was leaning forward in her chair, elbows on her knees, waiting for the next juicy tidbit.

"No, he didn't come in for dinner," I said. "I didn't see him the rest of the day."

"Wow," said Stefia. She sat back in her chair, chewing on her thoughts, replaying the story in her head. "So he was ignoring you because he liked you?"

"I don't think like was quite the right word," I said.

And in trying to decipher what word would have best explained the aggressive, all consuming, distraction that I was to Grant—or that Grant became for me—I was tossed back into the story and continued telling.

Thinking of Grant and the way he yelled at me to leave him in the machine shed always gave me shivers. And I really did my best to stay away from him. We had an unspoken agreement on boundaries, and an unspoken agreement not to cross them. And it worked out pretty well.

But in July of 1965 there was a summer storm that whipped up from nothing—black skies and torrential rain and wind like I'd never seen before and haven't ever since. I had run to town quick to get groceries, leaving the kids with Helmer at home. This storm blew in from nowhere. I was driving on the gravel right in front of Grant and Julie's farm and the road suddenly washed out. Grant saw the headlights of the car and came out to see who was stuck halfway in the ditch and realized it was me. It was pitch black, pouring down rain like something out of a movie and the wind was whipping tree branches across the road and he yelled at me, "Just come inside!"

I knew there wasn't anyone else home because Julie had taken the kids to her mother's house for the weekend. She'd told me that.

I knew Grant was there alone.

I was sopping wet standing in the rain. He said something that I didn't hear and then lightning struck a tree right next to us and I screamed.

"Anna Marie! Just come inside, for Christ's sake!"

And I thought about what he'd said before about not being alone with me and I thought about what I wanted and I prayed to every saint I knew that the wind would not come up and blow me the wrong way.

It didn't.

I looked at Stefia. She was holding her breath, waiting. Waiting. Wanting to know the next piece. Wanting to know which way the wind blew.

"James was born the following April," I said. And I smiled.

Stefia exhaled.

"Did Helmer ever know?" she asked, chewing on the edge of her thumbnail.

I shook my head.

"So he raised James as his own son?"

I nodded.

She flopped back in her chair.

"Oh my god, Anna Marie."

"See, we all have secrets. All of us."

"So," she continued, "if your husband never knew…who did you tell?"

I thought for a minute.

"As far as I know, Grant and I were the only people who ever knew. And at first he didn't even know. I think he just did the math and figured it out. He never came right out and said it, but I knew from the look in his eyes the first time he saw James. He knew."

"And how did he take it?"

I looked at my empty coffee cup. I traced the edge of it with my fingertip, thinking on that night during the storm when Grant had done the same with his fingertip along my cheek and around my mouth and over the point of my chin and down my neck…

"He was devastated. He was never the same after that. Never the same after he saw James for the first time. I think it just…crushed him."

"Wait a second. You're telling me no one else knew about this?" Stefia asked. "Why are you telling me about it?"

I kept tracing the coffee cup and thinking. And tracing. And thinking.

"I guess I told you because in the grand scheme of things, I don't really know you."

"I don't get it," she said. "That's totally counterintuitive, Anna Marie..."

"It's not. I've only known you for eight weeks, so really we're not that close. You're not close, so I can be honest," I said. "Stefia, the closer we get to people, the less we can share. Surely, you must know that."

"That doesn't make sense."

"That doesn't mean it's not true," I said. "I told you we all have secrets, Stefia. Every single one of us."

I was still tracing the rim of the coffee mug.

Still tracing.

Still tracing.

**

The ninth week Stefia came to visit she walked in with her thermos of coffee without saying a word. She poured two mugs, pushed one across the table to me, and sat down in the chair opposite where I was. She took in a deep breath. Then another.

Then she spoke.

"My mother left home when I was thirteen. I hated that day."

The time had come for Stefia to tell a story.

"I was really mad about it for a long time," she said.

"That's a hard thing to get over."

"I think the hardest thing was that no one knew where she went."

But there was a hitch in her breath. A catch. A skip. I watched Stefia's eyes and tried to read what was behind them.

"There's more to the story?" I asked.

"Why do you ask that?"

"I can see your eyes."

She took a deep breath. And then another.

"I've known where my mom was the whole time," Stefia finally said. "I found a note in a secret spot. There was a tree in our front yard that had a hollow spot in it. Mom and I built a tiny box one day and hid things in that box just as a game. Sometimes it was plastic little treasures, sometimes it was things we cut out from magazines, but most of the times it was notes."

"She hid a note in there for you when she left?"

"Well, I didn't know she had. I mean, initially. I didn't find it for two months. I didn't think about looking for anything when she first left because I thought she would come back."

"Did she leave many times before that?"

"No," Stefia said, looking at me as if I'd just asked her the most impossible thing. "She had never left. She was always home."

"How did you know she wasn't coming back?"

"Mail stopped coming to our house for her. I was old enough to figure out she'd had her address changed. So I figured that meant she'd ended up somewhere. And then I was brave enough to check that secret hiding spot."

"What did the note say."

"She'd moved to New York."

"New York?"

"Yeah. For the theater."

Outside my room, a young girl slowly passed by with a vending machine cup of hot cocoa. She alternated between blowing at the steam and sipping gingerly, trying to protect her taste buds as she indulged in the liquid chocolate.

"Before she met dad, she was big into theater," Stefia continued. "I mean, big time. The summer she met my father, she was supposed to be heading off to New York to audition for some company that had pretty much already promised her a spot. Two months later, when she was getting ready to leave, she found out she was pregnant with me."

The girl with the hot cocoa stopped in front of my room as if she was listening to the story. Stefia saw my eyes at the door and turned her head.

"Hello," she said to the girl. Stefia picked up her thermos and held it out. "Want some coffee?"

The little girl grinned, took another sip of her cocoa, and continued walking past my room.

"Anyway," Stefia resumed with a sigh, "at least that's what the note said. I didn't know any of that about my mom before I read that note."

Stefia didn't say anything else for a long time. She got out of her chair and looked at the old Polaroid snapshots I'd pegged up around my room. She picked up the scribbly Crayola drawings from great grandchildren that sat on my nightstand. She asked if I wanted more coffee and I shook my head.

"Stefia?"

"Yeah?"

"Is that why you decided to become an actress?"

"Huh?"

"Because of your mom?"

Stefia didn't say anything. She just looked at the black and white checkered floor and slipped the back of her shoe off and on, off and on.

"Well, anyway, you don't have to tell me anything," I said, finally. "You don't have to answer any questions you don't want to. That's our deal, right?"

"Yeah." Stefia smiled, checking her phone for the time.

"Did your dad know where she went?" I asked.

"My mom?"

"Yeah."

Stefia paused for a minute, and then cleared her throat as if she was trying to cough the answer out. "He was the one who told her to go," Stefia said. "That was in the note, too. Dad didn't want to keep mom from her dream."

"Her dream?"

"He felt like if she stayed with us, she'd be—how did it go?—*wasting her true purpose*." Stefia's voice turned sharp. "But I'm pretty sure dad doesn't know about that note under the tree."

"So your dad doesn't know that you know?"

"Nope."

A tiny smirk of irony slid across my lips. I knew why she was telling me instead of her dad. Because she'd only known me for nine weeks, and in the grand scheme of things, we didn't really know each other.

"We all have secrets" I said. "Don't we?"

And then Stefia smiled one of those smiles that made you feel less comfortable for having seen it.

"Anna? You know the answer to your question, right?"

"Which one?"

"The one about why I'm an actress?"

I thought for a minute.

"I don't have to answer that," I said. "That was our deal."

Stefia smiled.

And I knew.

We talked another fifteen minutes about everything except her mom and dad, instead flitting from the topic of aliens to drag racing to the best way to cook a steak. Then Stefia checked her phone again for the time and announced it was time to leave.

"You enjoy your day," I said and giggled, "and thanks again for the hot coffee. I so enjoy our visits."

"So do I, Anna Marie," she said. She took my ceramic mug from me and rinsed it in my bathroom sink. She dried it carefully and stuck it back in its hiding spot in the closet.

"For next time," she said. She smiled but it seemed to lack the glitter and gusto that usually lit up my room.

"Is something bothering you today, Stefia?" I asked.

"I'm just really tired," she said, then smirked. "I suppose you think that's silly. Like...how hard can acting be?"

I thought for a minute and answered carefully.

"Acting is one of the most exhausting things known to man. It's hard to be someone you're not. It takes a lot out of you."

"Yeah," she said, dismissively. She picked up her empty thermos and headed for the door.

"And Stefia?" I said.

"Yeah?"

"Being in a play is probably pretty hard, too."

Stefia smiled.

And I knew.

She knew that I knew.

And that's all that mattered.

**

I sit now in my pink room in a simple black dress, strangled by the irony that Stefia's funeral is on a Wednesday.

I throw my blue and green ceramic mug across the room and watch it shatter as it hits the wall.

Why did it have to be on a Wednesday?

Rowena hears the mug break all the way in the nurse's station and rushes to my room. She throws open my door so hard that the handle jams into the closet behind it.

"Anna Marie!" she says, stopping short of the broken pieces of mug scattered in the floor. "Oh my god, are you okay?"

I am not okay.

I am not okay.

And one thought consumes my mind as Rowena stares at me, her lips moving but no sound reaching my ears: I want to unknow everything that I know.

-Gabriella-

Words were my currency. As he pushed his way in and out of my mouth he filled me with words and I could finally explain the blunt square-headed ache that came when the drought shriveled the zucchini and my pants hung off my hips and mom left and never game back.

We lay together twisted up in sweaty sheets and I traced my finger along the outline of him. I wanted to slice my fingernail through his skin and down his arm; leave a trail that would bleed and scar. Just to prove to myself he was there. Just to prove he was real.

Please be here.

Sometimes I don't want Adam to talk. I don't want to hear the crackle-scratch-clip of his voice. Sometimes I just want to grab his face and claw my way through the skin of his cheeks. But other times I want to drag the soft of my lower lip just below his, catching the bristle of a four day beard on his chin.

Please. Be here.

I fish my palm up his arm through the sleeve of his t-shirt and out the neck hole, closing a fist around the fabric. I have him, or at least the cotton that covers him, firmly in my grasp.

In the dim glow of what light sneaks through the window, I see the edge of his lips twist into a grin.

"Why are you holding on so tight?" Adam asks.

"I want you here," I say.

"I am here."

"I want you to stay."

"I'm not leaving."

"But sometimes people do. Sometimes people say they're staying but they change their mind and don't change it back."

His grin fades into a crisp straight line and now he is serious. He rolls to face me full on and repeats in a thick voice I can latch on to:

"I'm not leaving."

I want to curl up in his words. I want to fix them around my shoulders and cover my neck and plug my ears with the things he says. His words are few but solid and sure. There is comfort in the sound of him and in the weight of them.

Please.

Be.

Here.

His gaze moves from me to the neat and crisp dress I've hung from a hanger on the hook over my door and I know he's saying without saying that we should really get ready to leave.

My look back to him says I don't want to.

If I go, I will be the girl in the corner, the girl in the shadow made by the cast of light her oldest sister throws off. There is no difference whether she is alive or dead. Stefia will always be the most brightly shining star in the room.

"Let's get ready," he breathes into my ear.

"I'm not going."

His lips open again and close gently on the top edge of my ear.

"Come on, Gabriella," he whispers. "You have to."

"I don't have to do anything."

"Oh, Gabriella…"

It almost sounds like he's pouting. I know he's tsk tsking me.

"I was hoping to see you in that dress you hung on the door," he continues.

"Liar," I say. "You're happiest when I'm not dressed at all."

"Wrong. I'm happiest just having you by me, whether you're clothed or not."

I stare at the popcorn textured ceiling of the hotel room we've woken up in and I wonder who laid in this bed before us? Were they happy? Did they make wild passionate love but never kiss on the lips? Were they comfortable in their nakedness or did she ask to turn off the lights? What kind of home did they return to? And did they return home together?

I close my eyes. I wonder why I wondered about it. I realize it doesn't matter.

"Gabriella, you have to go to the funeral," he says, and then as a correction, adds, "We have to go."

"No. We don't."

**

"Gabriella!" I can hear her laughing. I remember that day. I remember the one time we got away just us three sisters.

164

There was just over a year separating each of us by age and if we dressed just right we could almost get away with looking like triplets. So we all wore white skinny jeans and a solid color tank top, big matted brass hoops and knee high boots. We looked great, but Stefia looked best of all. She had a way of shining like a beacon even if we were all saying or doing or wearing the same thing.

We went to eat at McRudy's that day. Cokes and cheeseburgers and fries and then, because we were pretending it was our own personal Sister Thanksgiving, strawberry shakes. We walked out of McRudy's feeling like the buttons on our jeans would pop off and fly across the parking lot. We were so stuffed.

We laughed. Oh god, did we laugh. We laughed about funny things dad had said and stupid things mom had done. And remember that one Christmas when we went shopping but forgot to bring all the Christmas lists with so we just punted and ended up picking out the best gifts ever? That afternoon Stefia was my sister. She was just my sister, nothing else.

The only thing I ever wanted was for my sister to sit with me for a meal somewhere where no one else recognized her. Somewhere I could talk to her as my big sister. Somewhere that she could just be herself and not the person everyone else saw her as.

Just. My. Sister.

After McRudy's, we planned to see a movie. We rolled our stuffed bellies into Stefia's car. Stefia picked up her cell phone to check her messages and said, "Crap."

"What?" Naomi asked.

"I've got to take this message. Give me a second, okay?"

So Stefia got back out of the car, sent the number through on her phone, and walked away from the car to talk.

"Who is she talking to?" I asked, not hiding my annoyance. "The pope?"

"Who knows," Naomi said from the front passenger seat. "Don't be mad."

"She said this was just going to be a sister day. Now Hollywood calls and she's just going to ditch us?"

Naomi turned around.

"What is your problem? Who said Hollywood was calling? It could have been dad for all we know."

"If it were dad, she wouldn't have gotten out of the car to return the call."

"Maybe he was asking about a Christmas list. Maybe he was asking what Stefia had already bought someone and he didn't want you to know."

"Why couldn't she just text that back to him?"

"Gabriella, honestly," Naomi said, heaving out a sigh of exasperation. "What does it matter who is on the phone anyway?"

"Because this was just supposed to be a sister afternoon."

"Why can't you just be happy for her? I mean, Christ! She's practically a small town movie star."

"No, she's not," I said. "She's just my sister."

Naomi turned back around in the seat and looked out the windshield. She muttered something under her breath and shook her head.

"What?" I yelled.

"Nothing."

"No, tell me!"

Stefia was standing in front of the car, facing away from us but you could tell from the way she was holding her stomach that she was laughing.

"I just don't get why you have to be so bitter," Naomi said, not bothering to turn around and look at me. "It doesn't help her at all."

"Now I'm supposed to help her?" I said. "I don't know why she needs our help. She seems to be doing just fine on her own."

"It's not her fault that people think she's talented at what she does. Gabriella, she *is* talented. Don't you get that?"

"Yeah, I do. But so what?"

"So...I don't know why in the world that means you have to be mad at her. You're punishing her for something she has no control over."

"Bullshit," I said.

"What?"

"I said bullshit. I think she likes the fame."

"I didn't say she didn't. Who wouldn't? I said she can't control that people like her and want her to do stuff. I mean, the girl could read the back of a cereal box and people would fall down at her feet. I think that's pretty darn amazing."

"I think it's bullshit," I said, staring out my window. Stefia finished her phone call and opened the car door to hop back into the driver's seat.

"Sorry, gals," she said, bubbly as ever. "No more interruptions from now on."

"Who was that?" I asked.

"Dad. He thought we were going to be home by now. I asked him if he forgot we were catching the movie. He said he had, and was thinking maybe some group of men carried the three of us off. He was wondering if he needed to send out a SWAT team to find us."

Naomi and she collapsed into giggles in the front seat, squealing about dad and his overactive imagination, and Stefia started the car and steered it towards the movie theater.

But me? I wasn't laughing. Because I didn't believe that Stefia had been talking to dad. Stefia was an actress, master of making people believe all things. I imagined her as reading a script most of the time she was awake. Just reciting lines she was supposed to say.

I wished someone would have just written her a scene where she looked me in the eye and said, *Gosh, I'm so glad to be your sister. And you matter to me.*

Now that would have been a moving, emotional scene.

Too bad she never picked up that script.

**

Adam leans into my back with a gentle kiss, pressing his fingers into my shoulder.

"Are you coming?" he teases. "There's plenty of room in the shower for both of us…"

He tugs at the sheets, pulling them off slowly, leaving me more and more exposed as the bedding slips to the floor. I ignore him.

"Come on, Gabriella. You're going to get cold. Come conserve water in the shower with me."

I close my eyes and think of Stefia.

He stops tugging on the bedding, picks up one of the pillows and throws it at my head.

"Come on, Gabriella. It's not funny anymore. Get out of bed. We have to leave in an hour."

"Adam, I told you I'm not going."

He stands at the right hand side of the bed, hands on hips, still feeling smart for tossing the pillow that I didn't bother to move off my face where it landed.

"I already told you we have to go," he said. "What will people think if we don't?"

"Why do you care?"

"People will want you to be there."

"They never did before."

"What's that supposed to mean?"

"It means if they didn't care if I was around or not when she was alive, what the hell difference does it make now that she's dead?"

"You can't mean that."

"I do mean it."

His eyes would not divert from me, as if he was trying to see past my skin to determine if I was telling the truth.

"Well, I'm still going," he said.

"What?"

"I'm still going to the funeral."

"My family hardly knows you, Adam."

"It doesn't matter. I'm going to pay my respects to the dead."

"What's that supposed to mean?"

"Just what I said."

He picks up the bedding off the floor, sets it back up on the mattress, and walks around the bed to pick the pillow up that he tossed.

"You will regret not going to her funeral," he said, brushing my hair out of my face.

"I have never regretted anything I've done except for not being born first."

He stares at me. His eyes beat through my skin and make the hairs on my neck stand up. Suddenly I'm cold.

"I'm getting in the shower," he says finally. "If you change your mind about getting ready to go, you know where I'll be."

I don't respond. I just watch him walk into the bathroom and pull the door almost shut, just enough so it doesn't quite latch.

An invitation.

One I will decline.

I've spent my life living in someone else's shadow. I've spent my life wondering why doing the right things didn't get me the all-adoring eyes that my sister seemed to attract just by breathing. The blood pumping through her body was enough to make people flat out stupid with undeserved respect for something anyone could have done just as well as her if she only would have sat down long enough for someone else to try.

I hear the water turn on and splash at the floor of the shower. Adam hums a nameless tune.

My eyelids close and in my head I hear six gunshots. Six lifeless bodies breaking and slumping to the floor. I hear the squishing and pumping of Stefia's heart slowing. I hear her breath choking. I hear the chaos of gurgling and sputtering. I hear screams that are fading....fading...fading...

How is it that even after the light has gone out, she still manages to shine? How is it that in her death, she's still more important than anything else that's alive?

I'm not going to the funeral. I knew that when we got on the plane to come here. And I haven't changed my mind.

I'm not going.

I'm not going.

I'm not going.

And then I can hear her voice. Her gurgling sputtering voice that's choking on blood. Suddenly she's not so pretty anymore. Suddenly she's not the gorgeous supermodel type angel up on a pedestal. She's fallen and is just lying in a pool of her own fluid.

Please. Be here, she says.

I'm not going.

I want you here, she says.

I'm not going.

Please don't leave. I need you here.

I'm not going, Stefia.

Please. Be. Here.

No.

-Paul-

Community theater doesn't just attract actors living in the immediate community. Every actor has a checklist of roles on their bucket list; Simon Bradford Collins from *Don't Mind If I Do* was in my top three. So when the Crystal Plains Theater announced they were holding auditions for it last summer—directed by David Jeffery Hank, no less—I figured it was totally worth the hour and twenty minute drive to try my luck.

Last summer was the first time Crystal Plains decided to do two summer shows. Both were smaller productions involving less people and cost, but it was a great way to toss up the palette of theater goers in the area. They chose one family oriented show for the beginning of the summer, and ran an edgier show for the second half.

Don't Mind If I Do was the edgier show. Some people thought it was too sinful for Granite Ledge to do. One of those "if you aren't old enough to drive yourself to the show, you probably shouldn't be in the audience when it's running" kind of deals. But the two guys who started up the theater, Niles and James, knew how to make waves. It's how they sold tickets. When someone from the local paper interviewed Niles about the questionable nature of the show they had chosen, Niles simply grinned and said, "If people don't want to see it, by all means, stay home."

Anyway, so I auditioned. And there were two surprises that happened. The first surprise being that I actually got cast in the role I wanted. The second surprise was that a 16 year old was cast opposite me, in a role meant for someone almost twice her age.

Now, at the time of the show, I was twenty-four. I wasn't far off from Simon's actual age of twenty-eight. But a sixteen-year-old in the role of twenty-eight-year-old Kate? I wanted to ask David why he hadn't closed the auditions to minors, but you really shouldn't bite the hand that feeds you.

So I showed up a few minutes early to the first full cast read through, and made small talk with the director trying to get a sense of what to expect from this Stefia before I met her.

"So…sixteen?" It was all I could think of to say.

175

"She's almost seventeen," David said. "Don't let her age scare you off. I mean, I get it. I do. But really, she's ah-ma-zing."

He said it just like that: ah-ma-zing. And I figured she better be good, causing a grown man to talk like a total idiot and all.

"Trust me," he continued, with an easy smile, "I'm the director. I know what I'm doing."

And while I was wondering what I could say to back pedal so he wouldn't worry about having issues between the two leads, Stefia walked in.

Shit.

Not that Stefia looked like she was sixteen. Because if you wouldn't have told me otherwise, I would have assumed I could have taken her out for drinks after our read through. And not that she acted like she was sixteen. Because all she had to do was open her mouth and you'd have figured she was working on her PhD in Psychiatry. But she *was* sixteen. Like...eight years younger than me. In high school. Just starting to drive by herself. I had friends who were getting married and having kids...and the director wanted me to act out those crazy scenes against a sixteen-year-old?

Shit.

She was gorgeous. And when she opened her mouth for lines at that read through I probably looked like she'd hit me in the chest. I mean, a person could happily choke listening to the thick velvet ribbons that spun from her lips.

But she was sixteen.

Sixteen. Sixteen. Sixteen.

***

Anyone who tells you that what happens on stage is just pretend has never been on stage. I mean, it is pretend, it's not real life…and yet it is its own kind of reality. Like being on stage is its own world, where the rules don't matter. Relationships between actors in a play are deep and unexplainable. I mean, you're not together…but you are. You're more together on stage than you are with anyone in real life. There's only so much acting that goes into making something believable…and the rest is real. You pour yourself into a role and you leave a part of yourself there. You get so deep into your character's head that at some point it's not possible to completely come back out.

I knew my last scene of the play was going to be rough to block. My character had to toss Stefia's character around the stage like she was a ragdoll and have his way with her. It wasn't just a quick thing, either. It was this scene that went on and on.

Stefia was only sixteen.

"Okay," David said, sitting the two of us down before blocking. "Here's the deal. This is a big scene. This is a huge scene. And this is one of those scenes an actor could get injured in."

"Well, block it the right way so we don't, David," Stefia teased.

"Follow the blocking and you'll be fine," he corrected. "It's easy to get lost in what's happening and find yourself out of control."

"You're the director," Stefia said, with a polite curtsey. "We are your loyal servants."

I snorted and gave David a sweeping bow, adding, "Good sir, we are here to do your will."

"Okay, you guys," David laughed. "I get it."

David walked us through where he wanted us to stand, where he wanted us to move, what he had envisioned for the scene and how he thought it would play itself out. Lots of times he would give a direction, and then look to Stefia to see her reaction. Like then Paul is going to jump on top of you and straddle you with his knees... I mean, she was the sixteen-year-old, right? We had to be careful with her.

We tried it a few times, at every rehearsal, but it didn't feel right. I thought once we were off book and weren't fumbling with a script, it would get better, but it didn't. It felt weird. It felt fake. And I knew it wasn't right because David looked so tentative. He walked around the stage, rubbing his chin with his fingers, then he poked at his temples. He sighed three times before he said anything.

"You've got to let go," he finally said to me. "You're holding back."

He was right. I was.

"I don't want to hurt her," I said. "I've never had to act a scene like this. How do you make this believable without causing actual pain?"

"I'll let you know if it's too much," Stefia interrupted. "I'm not little. I'm not weak."

"I'm not saying you are, I'm just…"

"Trust me. I'll let you know."

"But how are you going to let me know? If you say stop or you're hurting me or don't do that I'm going to assume that's all part of your ad-libbed lines."

"It helps to have a code," David suggested. "Something that has nothing to do with lines so you won't get confused that she's ad-libbing. Maybe an action, but not something that's obvious to the audience if it happens. So…think on that, okay?"

"Okay," we said at the same time.

"Now, let's run it once more," David said. "And this time, I want you both to let go. I challenge you to try and make me stop the scene because it's too much."

Stefia grinned and said, "I'm always up for a challenge."

And so we took it. At first it was hard to get into that hardcore character. There's something embarrassing about being that physically violent—or physically vulnerable— when someone is watching. But we kept at it. Stefia's eyes encouraged me to keep going, giving me a power that I wouldn't have known I could even pretend to have. David just kept watching intently and nodding, so I knew we were getting closer.

By the time the scene ended, Stefia had smacked me in the face, I had called her a few names that weren't in the script, and we were both breathing so hard I thought she was going to pass out.

I looked up.

David smiled.

"You're getting there," he said. "That was a huge improvement."

I smiled.

"Was that okay for you, Stefia?" David asked.

She was still sitting on the floor by the bed where scene had ended, trying to catch her breath. But she nodded at David.

"Positive?" I asked, putting my hand out in front of her to help her up.

"Yes," she said, pushing herself up on her own. "Positive."

She stood up, gave me a quick smile, and straightened her clothes.

I got it. We'd keep it professional. In a role like that, it was easier for us to not get involved too much with each other. The better I knew her, the harder it would be to toss her around.

And besides, she was only sixteen.

**

After the last dress rehearsal, everyone went to a little place in town called Beidermann's. Tradition, Stefia said. Burgers, fries, and shakes all on Niles' and James' tab.

"Nice guys, paying for all that," I said, sitting by Stefia and waiting for our food.

"They've got money."

"Are they a couple?"

"Oh, god. No," she laughed. "James is married to Mary. Niles and them all went to college together. Theater geeks from the beginning."

"Theater geeks...with money." I laughed. "Is Niles married?"

She turned to take her food from the waitress who was balancing all of our food on one tray.

"Niles? No. Not married. Why?"

"Just trying to figure this whole theater group out," I said, taking my own plate as Stefia passed it to me. "I'm not from around here, you know. Kind of seems like everyone knows everyone and everything about them, except for me."

"You're an implant."

"An outsider," I said, putting my hands up and wiggling my fingers like I was talking about a ghost.

"But that's okay," she said. "And besides. Not everyone knows everyone here. Or everything about them."

"Oh, come on," I said, taking a fry and pushing it through the puddle of ketchup I had squirted on my plate. "This is small town America."

"People still keep secrets," she said, and when I raised a doubtful eyebrow, she continued. "Okay. See the table over there?"

Stefia pointed at a teenaged couple sitting against the opposite wall. They were eating ice cream cones and laughing.

"First date?" I said.

"Nope. They've been dating six months."

"They look happy."

"She's pregnant. Just found out a month ago."

"Oh?"

"It's not his."

"Oh."

"He doesn't know."

"Wait. He doesn't know she's pregnant or he doesn't know that it's not his?"

"Neither," she said. "He doesn't know either thing."

I wagged my head with an I-told-you-so smile.

"See, Stefia? That's what I mean. This is small town. You know lots about lots of people. Everything about everyone, that's how small towns work."

She took a bite of her burger and then wiped a drip of mustard off her chin.

"But that guy with Miss Pregnant?" she said, pointing back at the couple. "He doesn't know the biggest important news about her. Get it? Not everyone here knows everything about everyone."

"I thought everyone in small towns liked to talk."

"Oh, they do. But they also know how to keep secrets."

The waitress brought our shakes and we all moved to make room for them on the table.

"Mmm, chocolate," Stefia said when she sucked some of hers up the straw. "My favorite."

"You know, you should really cut out of this little town," I said.

"And go where?"

"Somewhere with a bigger theater district."

"Oh. Sure. New York, where everyone's dreams are chewed up and spit out."

"No, not New York," I said, shaking my head. "New York is too cutthroat. Everything they say about New York is true. You never get a chance to do a show. But there are a billion other hubs for theater around the country. I mean, even just head down to Minneapolis…"

"Or I could just stay here."

"Why?"

"Why not?"

"Because you're really talented and they need people like you there."

She shook her head and took another pull off her shake.

"Come on, Paul. You expect me to believe you don't say that to all your leading ladies?"

"I don't. I promise."

"Paul, seriously."

"Listen," I said. I set my shake down and turned my chair to face her. "Look at me."

She turned to look at me with a grin, but then saw how serious I was and her smile faded. "You're a really talented actress. You're good." Then I leaned in closer by her ear and whispered, "You're way better than everyone in this show. Shit, you're better than me…"

"I am not."

"I'm serious," I said, sitting back in my chair

She smiled half-heartedly, but did not look away.

"That's called a compliment, by the way. You need to learn how to take a compliment."

"I'm fine with compliments," she said, finally turning back to the table and swirling her straw in her shake. "I'm just not a fan of the strings that are often attached to them."

I took my last fry and shoved it in my mouth.

"I just think you're talented," I said, "and I thought you should know. No strings attached."

"Okay," she smiled. "Thank you for the string-less compliment."

She was gorgeous and she was sixteen and she was ah-mazing. No strings attached.

**

The opening night crowd for *Don't Mind If I Do* was almost sold out. We figured that had something to do with all the local press talking up the sinful nature of the show, and Niles telling people to stay home if they didn't want to see it.

An hour and seventeen minutes into the show, my big scene began. It started by me shoving her across the stage. She completed a well-blocked trip and fell on the ground, which wasn't hard because my nerves had caused me to push her harder than normal. Then I sauntered over to her, kicked at her side and told her to get up. I screamed a ton of disgusting things at her, lines that you wouldn't believe someone could actually put in a script, and yet if they were anything different, you'd call the entire scene unbelievable.

 I grabbed her by the arm and dragged her kicking and screaming over to a dresser next to the bed. More lines were tossed out. We both blared and shrieked at each other until it seemed the stage lights might fall down on top of us. A few cast members off stage were watching, one stagehand biting her fingernails. I mean, biting her fingernails even after she'd watched it at least twenty-five times in rehearsal? Opening night made everything way more intense. It was the lights, the audience…everything.

Two minutes and a bunch of dialogue into our scene, Stefia's character was supposed to start fighting back. And I don't know if it was nerves or what but she gave it all she had. And the more she gave, the harder I fought her. We got into it something serious. She was fighting back and I was fighting her and I wondered for a second if we weren't acting anymore.

It was then I realized we'd never figured out the code to tell each other we'd gone too far. I mean, we had been following the blocking exactly, but everything seemed more sharp and vivid than it had ever been in rehearsal.

What was it David had said? These were the scenes when actors get lost in what's happening and lose control? Everything was different with an audience. When people watched, it multiplied everything you did by a million.

I grabbed her by the neck and looked into her eyes. I searched for something on her face that said what we were doing was still okay. I pushed her backwards onto the bed. She flipped over and tried to crawl away on her hands and knees but I grabbed her by the ankles, pulled her towards me and turned her onto her back.

She is sixteen.

She is sixteen.

She is sixteen.

I was supposed to tear her costume right down the front of her. There were two reasons this was supposedly okay. First, since the bedding was positioned just so, and because of how she was blocked to lay on the bed as this happened, the audience would never see any nudity from Stefia. David had assured her of that multiple times. Secondly, her costume was specially made so that no matter how hard I tore the fabric, it would only rip down to a certain point. Which meant I would see minimal nudity, if any, from Stefia.

That's how it was supposed to go.

She lay on the bed, still acting as though she was trying to get away, and I climbed on top of her, straddling her between my knees. I grabbed at the neckline of her costume and tore with the same force I'd torn in all the dress rehearsals.

I swear. I did.

But the tear didn't stop. It went right past the fabric panel that was sewn in to stop the tear.

Now, Stefia was on the bed and the audience couldn't see what I saw. None of the other actors or stage hands could see what I saw. David Jeffery Hank couldn't see what I saw.

What I saw was the word *Hate*. Right there, etched in thick, puffy red letters into the skin below her breasts.

Hate.

She was a cutter.

Stefia realized I'd seen it about the same time I realized what it was and for a millisecond we were thrown right out of the scene. I stared into her eyes and saw a mixture of anger and fear and almost an apology for having put it there to be seen. You could have heard a pin drop; the silence was closing in on my ears, louder than any applause I'd ever heard in my life.

David had blocked the end of the scene to be absolute physical chaos. But I didn't want that for Stefia. Not that night, anyway.

Instead, I held her arms above her head and pinned to the bed. Then I got close to her ear and whispered *stop fighting*.

She did.

So I traced my finger over the tip of her nose, down her neck, and between her breasts that were barely covered with a white lace bra. I closed my fingers and rested my hand over the word hate.

Then I saw a tear form in the corner of her eye.

I saw Trevor off stage getting ready to enter stage right for his part which was to pull me off of her, and I knew our improvisation was almost over. There had been no kissing blocked into our scene, but I decided at that moment to kiss her harder than I've ever kissed anyone in my life before or since, like an apology for whatever she was going through that made her slice hate into her chest. The kiss lingered and my tongue slid its way into her mouth.

She kissed me back. I know she returned the kiss.

And then she bit my tongue.

She bit my fucking tongue as hard as she could.

Trevor ran in to pull me off of Stefia and was supposed to toss me with a well-blocked shove out the door stage left. But I was so caught off guard at the kiss, the bite, and that I could taste blood that I tripped and cracked my hand against the doorframe so hard that I wondered if the audience knew it was an accident.

I stumbled into the wings, catching myself by the curtain and sat down, cradling my hand. Oh, my god…the fucking pain…

Henny, the stagehand came running over.

"Is it broken, man? Did you break it?"

"I…I don't know," I said. "Just let me sit here a minute. I don't feel good…"

Henny ran to get David. I laid my head back against the heavy curtain and closed my eyes. My heart was pounding. I was going to pass out. I felt like shit.

I knew it didn't have anything to do with my hand.

**

After wincing my way through a bow that night, it came to our attention Dr. Patton was in the audience. He came backstage to look at my hand and assured me it wasn't broken. I went into the guys' dressing room and sat with an ice pack because I needed to sit.

I just wanted to sit and think.

David came in to check on my hand, again. He commented that our fight scene was the best he'd ever witnessed, the most ah-ma-zing ever, and congratulated me for really throwing myself into it. But I could also tell he was paranoid that I was going to be mad for the injury. I figured it must be hard to be a director because on one hand, he was pleased the scene had been so intense and convincing, but he wasn't stupid and he could tell something had caused that scene to be what it was.

I assured him it was fine, it would heal, and that I was completely okay to do the rest of the nine shows we had scheduled.

"I wasn't talking about your hand," he said.

Stefia walked in. David looked at her, then back at me. I hadn't told him anything about what led to the most amazing scene ever on stage, but he knew by the heavy air between Stefia and I that we needed to clear something up.

"You okay, kid?" he asked Stefia.

"I'm fine," she said, "and you know I'm not a kid."

David smiled at the both of us, went to the door, looked back one more time, and finally left.

I looked down at the floor while rubbing my thigh with my good hand.

She said nothing. And after a full minute of silence, I couldn't stand it anymore.

"Okay. What was that?" I asked.

"What was what?"

"Come on. Don't play games."

Her eyes were so pristine, so faultless, that I almost wondered if maybe the whole thing had just been a case of two actors getting caught up in what was happening on stage.

But then there was a snag in her breath. Just the slightest slip. And I knew I hadn't misread anything.

"You're a cutter."

She breathed in, slowly.

"Why are you a cutter?"

She breathed out, slowly.

"Why did you bite me?"

Still, no answer.

"Stefia, you obviously came in here for a reason, and it wasn't just to stare at me. So say something."

"I bit you to distract you," she finally said.

"From what?" I said. "My lines? The blocking? The fact we were on stage?"

"The cutting. I knew from the look on your face you saw it. You weren't supposed to see it. How is your hand?"

"Don't worry about my hand," I said.

"Can we talk about something else?"

I stared at her in disbelief.

"Paul," she said, quickly, "I need you to not tell anyone about what you saw..."

"Why are you cutting?" I interrupted.

"I can't talk to you about this."

"Then what did you come in here for?"

She stopped and I watched as her gaze fell down the length of the dressing room table. The stage makeup was lined up in boxes, mostly cleaned up and put back where it was supposed to go for the next night's performance. She started fiddling with the things in the boxes, stacking cakes of foundation and putting tubes of mascara into the cup that kept them separated.

"Just please don't tell anyone what you saw," she said, without looking away from the makeup.

"Stefia, why do you do it?"

"Have you ever wanted to dig something out of your life?" she said, looking up at herself in the mirror. "Ever wanted to get rid of something that you knew wasn't yours to get rid of?"

I didn't respond. I just kept looking right at her, hoping she would look at me.

"If you can't get rid of that thing," she continued, "if you can't dig it out or cut it up…"

"I get it," I said. "If you can't cut that thing out of your life…you just cut yourself. I get it."

"You do?"

"My sister was a cutter."

"Then why did you ask why I did it?"

"What is the thing you want to get rid of that you can't? That's what I wanted to know."

"You don't get it," she said, shaking her head and biting at her top lip. "I can't tell people the truth. I can't."

"Just open your fucking mouth and say something. You do it all the time on stage."

"I read lines, Paul. That's all I do."

"What do you want to say that you can't say? Just open your mouth!"

"You are not pulling me into this," she said, coming right at me and pushing a finger at my face. "I did not ask for you to see those marks."

"But they are there, Stefia. They are there and I did see them and someone else besides me is going to see them. You're going to get measured for a costume or go skinny dipping at the beach or god knows what else and someone is going to see them."

"And then what?" she said, raking her fingers through her sweaty, over sprayed hair. "Paul, nobody is going to see them!"

"Yes, they will," I said, standing up and pointing at her. "And you know what? They're going to care enough to say something."

"Why would they care?"

I stared at her incredulously, wondering if her callous detachment from what she was saying was for real or just a front.

"Why *wouldn't* they care?"

"Listen, I'm sorry you saw it. This is...what you saw is the first thing I've cut. It's not a big deal."

"It is a big deal, and I will bet you every dollar I have that it's not the first time. Don't lie to me..."

"I don't owe you the truth," she hissed, stepping closer to me so no one would heard us outside the door. "I don't owe you anything. We just have to get through this run of shows and then you can go back to your big fancy ass theater in the cities and you never have to deal with me again. You don't have to worry about it."

"That's not the first carving you've done," I said, ignoring her outburst.

"It's the first *word*," she said, as if her correction meant anything.

"Why did you carve *hate?*"

"You wouldn't get it..."

"Try me."

"Why? Why the hell should I tell you anything?"

"Because we have to get through this run and then I can go back to my big fancy ass theater and not have to deal with you or worry about you. So why don't you just go ahead and tell me why you carved *hate?*"

She pulled at a stack of three rubber bands wound around her wrist, itching the mark the elastic had worn into her skin. Her jaw was locked in an attempt to squash back anything else that should never have come out. She stared. She focused her fiery little eyes right onto mine and finally unhinged her jaw.

"I carved *hate* because when I scratch at the surface of myself, that's what comes out."

There were no magical words I could conjure up to hurl out of my mouth at her to make the situation any better. The first time I'd seen her, I saw a put together, happy, absolutely beautiful woman who was sixteen, but so not sixteen. Now I just saw a churning ball of pain whose acidic insides were seeping out.

Of course. It's always the ones you don't suspect. Just like my sister.

David announced himself with a knock on the door and then walked in.

"Everything okay in here?"

"Fine," we both answered as shortly as we could. Stefia stared at her bare feet and I fixated on the throbbing in my hand.

"Listen, guys…if we need to change the scene…I mean….if it's too much…"

197

"It's not too much," Stefia said, emphatically. She looked up at David, took a deep breath, and then plastered a smile on her face. "It's not too much. It's perfect the way it is."

"It's only opening night, you guys," he said. "You've got nine more shows. I mean, the performance was amazing but...geez. I don't know if I can take nine more times of you guys freaking out..."

"Who said we're freaking out?" I asked.

"We're fine," Stefia said. "It's fine."

"I heard voices in here. I heard you..."

"It has nothing to do with the scene," Stefia said.

"Completely unrelated," I agreed.

If we would have been in a movie right then, the camera would have panned around to show each of our faces individually, fraught with worry. Then it would have fallen back to see the three of us in the dressing room in an uncomfortable dance of who was going to be the next person to speak up.

"No issues I need to worry about, then?" David finally asked.

"None," Stefia answered quickly, her eyes rising to meet mine.

"Everything is fine," tumbled out of my mouth, even though it was a total lie.

David walked out closed the door.

"So, let me get this right," I said. "Basically, you just want me to pretend I didn't see anything. You want me to pretend there is nothing wrong."

"Yeah," she said, full of sarcasm. "Gosh, I know. It's crazy. I'm asking you to act."

"Stefia, I'm not on a fucking stage right now..."

Hot stinging tears washed over my eyes. I wanted to break the mirror. I wanted to...

"God, Paul. Don't you get it?" she said, with a tired sigh.

"Get what?" I screamed.

"We're always on stage. Always."

She walked out of the dressing room and I kicked over the chair I'd sat in, sending it towards the door that she'd closed. I balled up two fists to hit the mirror but stopped short as pain stabbed through my hand, reminding me I'd already screwed it up enough.

Then the tears spilled over, hot and fast, and I didn't even bother to wipe them away. Do you know why? Because Stefia was right.

She was absolutely right.

We are never *not* on stage.

-Raynee-

Stefia was a train wreck waiting to happen.

Well, actually a car wreck, like when Old Man Rogers barreled his big ass farm truck down Main Street and plowed into that little car. But everyone always calls a bad situation a train wreck, so I've always thought of Stefia like a train.

So, train wreck. Car wreck. Whatever. It's like seeing something coming and knowing it's going to be bad. Knowing its coming, watching the disaster happen, wanting to look away, but not being able to. Just like when I was coming out of the drug store that one day a couple years ago and saw the mess Old Man Rogers made. It was horrible but we all just kept staring at the wreck.

Staring. Watching.

That's why I always kept watching Stefia. Princess Stefia. That annoying puke of small town royalty who got anything she wanted by twirling her perfect hair around her perfect finger. I'd kept watching her because I knew she was going to wreck.

"What do you have against her?" Gabriella had asked one afternoon. School had ended two hours prior, after which we walked to Beidermann's Ice Cream and decided to order double chocolate cones. We'd finished them and then hiked down to the river that the shop overlooked.

"She's everywhere. She's in everything. She's annoying," I said. I sucked on my cigarette and then turned my hand to look at the chipped nail polish on my thumbnail. I had painted lime green and black stripes on the nails of my right hand the night before bed and the polish hadn't even lasted twenty-four hours.

Cheap polish, I suppose, for a cheap girl.

"She's such a spoiled brat," Gabriella continued. "Which is kind of unfair, since I'm the youngest."

Gabriella was two years younger than me but cool as hell. Crazy, since she was also Stefia's youngest sister. Gabriella and I didn't talk to each other much during the school day but usually ended up doing something together after class let out.

"Everyone likes her," I said. "Stefia, I mean."

"Well, that's not a reason to not like her."

"What? Now you're part of the Princess Stefia club? I thought you couldn't stand your sister."

Gabriella laughed and pulled out a cigarette of her own. She lit it with her neon pink Bic and leaned her back against the giant boulder we were next to.

"No, I'm not part of her fan club," she said. "Let's make sure we have that clarified."

"Good."

"But if you're going to hate her, hate her because she's a stuck up bitch. Don't just hate her because she's got everyone else fooled about it."

I smirked and took one last drag off my cigarette and flicked the butt into the river.

"I've got plenty of reasons not to like your sister," I said. "And none of them have to do with what anyone else thinks about her."

"Oh yeah? Like what?"

"It all boils down to the fact that she's not for real."

And that was the truth. My whole issue with Stefia was that she seemed too perfect. Her life was too perfect. And perfect is a lie, everyone knows that.

She was hiding something.

"Are you going to Jimmy's birthday party this Saturday?" I asked.

"Yeah. I am. I mean, who isn't?" Gabriella smirked and lazily tossed a pebble in front of her. "I'm leaving with Adam afterwards."

"For the night?"

"No. For good. I'm done with this town."

"Don't you think someone will try and stop you?" I asked.

"Who would try to do that?" She picked up another rock, rolled it between her fingers, and then tossed it as hard as she could at the water.

I knew who wouldn't be at Jimmy's party. Stefia. Stefia never came to parties. Stefia was too good for high school parties. I didn't understand how the same person who didn't come to high school parties for whatever reason could still be worshipped by the same people she wouldn't party with.

Oh, to lie prostrate at the feet of Saint Stefia. To wrap oneself in adoration and adulation for the Princess of Perfection.

Well, fuck them.

**

That Saturday night, while marbling my nails blaze orange and yellow, I thought about Stefia and the homeroom class we shared as freshmen. I'd just moved to town and she was that goody-two-shoes who took it upon herself to welcome me.

"Welcome to Granite Ledge!" she had said, arm extended waiting for me to shake her hand. All I could think was what fourteen-year-old girl shakes hands? And as I sat there trying to figure out if it was a small town thing, or just something strictly Stefia (what kind of a name is that anyway?), she put her hand down and flitted away to grab another group of gals to introduce to the New Girl.

I tried as best as I could to peg Stefia down, fit her into a group. Was she a cheerleader? Was she student council president? Was she a recovering emo? As hard as I tried, I couldn't label her as anything. She was like a ridiculously gorgeous, unidentifiably shaped peg that wouldn't fit into any hole I wanted to slam her into.

A couple months after I started at the new school, I was hiding out and smoking a cigarette behind the bump out the lunch room made into the parking lot. School had been done for twenty minutes and I marveled at how quickly the parking lot had emptied. As I scanned the horizon, I realized Perky Perfect Stefia was getting into an old olive green Cutlass that had pulled up to the curb. I squinted to get a better look at her, wondering why the hell I found her so fascinating. She was like a magnet, this girl, and as I looked in the car I realized it might have had something to do with her daddy driving the car. Let me tell you, her dad was smoking hot.

A few weeks later, while hanging out with the only group I'd found to identify with, I said, "So. This Stefia girl."

The other girls looked at me.

"What about her?" asked Charlene.

"What's her story?" I asked.

"What do you mean? She ain't got a story. She's just...Stefia."

"Everyone has a story," I said. "Everyone has some dirt."

"Not Stefia," Charlene said. "She's just Stefia. She's always been Stefia. Parents had a little trouble beginning of this year...I think her mom walked out and left her dad but no one knows where she went. Hasn't seemed to trouble Stefia much. She lets most everything roll right off her back."

"She's an actress," another gal named Miggy said. "She got in with that theater on the edge of town and I guess she's pretty good."

"Does she act here at school?" I asked, marveling at the thought that a fourteen-year-old girl would be such an asset in community theater.

"We don't do much theater here until high school," said Charlene. "Don't have anyone to run the program. Lots of interest, but no one to hold it together."

"Well, regardless of what her story is…all I can say is her dad is pretty effin' hot. Bummer that her mom left, she must not have eyes in her head to see what was in front of her."

They looked at me like I had ten fingers coming out of my nose.

"Stefia's dad?" Miggy said. "Oh my god!"

"Oh, come on," I said. "He's hot! Tall? Dark hair cut super short? Just enough scruff on his face? Looks killer in a pair of sunglasses…"

Miggy snorted from where she sat cross-legged in the grass.

"Stefia's dad? He's not tall. Or dark-haired. And he's definitely not cute. Sunglasses or not."

"Are you sure?" I asked.

"I used to hang out with Stefia in third grade," Miggy said. "Her dad is about five foot ten on a good day and he's a ginger."

"Maybe it was an uncle?" I muttered to myself.

"Who was an uncle?" Miggy said.

"I just saw her getting picked up the other day after school and the guy who was driving was drop dead gorgeous. Just assumed it was her dad and figured that's why she is the way she is. You know, gorgeous and all? My bad, I guess."

I finished my cigarette and locked my mind around discovering who the gorgeous older guy was that Stefia got to ride around with.

As luck would have it, three days later, I was staked out in my hiding spot and the olive green Cutlass pulled up again. I snuck another peek at the guy and thought, man. How come freshman guys can't look like that? Shit, I didn't even know many seniors who looked that good.

I took my phone out of my pocket and zoomed in to get a real good look at this guy. If I took a picture, I could show the girls and they could tell me who it was. Everyone in small town Minnesota knows everyone else, right? I needed to know who this guy was.

As I zoomed in more and waited for the focus to sharpen, the gorgeous guy leaned over to Stefia to say something.

Focusing...focusing...

Then, I kid you not, after he scanned the parking lot to make sure it was empty, he leaned over further...and kissed Stefia.

On the lips.

I just about dropped my phone. And I forgot all about taking a picture.

Okay. Not her dad. And not her uncle.

Well, hopefully not.

**

A week or so later, I watched over Stefia's shoulder as she concentrated on making a precise incision into the pig fetus our group was dissecting in Biology for our year end project.

"Stefia," I said quietly, over her shoulder. "Do you walk home?"

"Usually," she said, not looking up.

"What do you do when it rains?"

"I get a ride."

"From who?" I asked. "Your dad?"

"God, no," she said, setting down one scalpel and picking up another. "My dad works an hour and a half away and doesn't get home until, like, 7:30. He's not around to give me a ride."

"Who gives you a ride?"

"Why?" she asked. "Do you need a ride after school?"

"Nope."

She set her knife down and turned over her shoulder to look at me.

"So why were you asking?"

"Just curious," I lied. "Thought I saw you yesterday walking by my house after school, but it must have been someone else."

"Well, it definitely wasn't me yesterday," she said, turning back to the pig fetus on the table. "Yesterday, I got a ride."

"That's weird," I said, walking around the table to look directly at her.

"Why?"

"Because it didn't rain yesterday."

She stared at the table, scalpel in hand, and slowly exhaled through her nose with more force than should have been necessary. Then she looked up at me with an icy glare. Her silence told me I was asking about things I should have known to leave alone.

It was then, the second week from the end of 9th grade that I decided Perfect Perky Princess Stefia might have been holing up a whole lot of stuff.

And it was then, the second week from the end of 9th grade that Stefia had figured out that I knew.

**

Later that Saturday night, I took my marbled nails, skinny jeans, and almost see through concert tee to Jimmy's party, fully prepared to have an amazing time. Jimmy said he was going to have a case of birthday cake vodka in honor of turning eighteen and said he'd save a special shot for me.

"Raynee!" everyone howled when I walked in. It was nice to be liked. It was nice to be the life of the party. It was nice to be the fun girl. I grabbed a beer and headed out to the balcony where Jimmy was sitting on the ledge waiting for me.

"Happy Birthday," I said, winding my arms around his waist. We were not dating. But he was hot and we were both there which was sometimes all that mattered.

"I've got something for you," he said, holding up the shot glass.

"I've got something better for you…" I said, locking my lips on his face and playfully running my fingertips over the front of his jeans.

"Okay," he said. I led him into the nearest room and closed the door.

Five minutes later I walked into the hallway, smoothing my hair in a pathetic attempt to look innocent as I rejoined the crowd. But the balcony was empty and quite a commotion had stirred up below in Jimmy's huge entry way.

"Jimmy, come out here!" I called, and then we quickly made our way down the stairs to where a small crowd had gathered.

I couldn't believe it. I couldn't fucking believe it.

Stefia had come to the party.

No one else could believe it either. Some people were so in shock they didn't know what to say, others fell all over themselves trying to be the first to bring a her a Solo cup of beer.

Like a goddamn celebrity.

I moved over to where a makeshift bar had been set up, with bottles of just about everything you could think of, and downed two shots of birthday cake vodka.

"Hey! Stefia!" I yelled, waving her over. "Come here!"

I smiled. I waved.

But she wouldn't come over.

I strained my ears to hear her conversation as she mingled, catching pieces of *anyone seen Gabriella* and *planning to skip town* and *I need to talk to her* as she moved through the crowd.

Most people ignored her questions and instead offered her a beer. She always refused.

Bitch.

She was deep in conversation with some girl when I stumbled on purpose in between them and spilled a whole Jagbomb all over the front of Stefia's shirt.

"Oh, god! I'm sorry!" I said. "I didn't mean to…"

Someone immediately brought Stefia a towel which she used to mop at her shirt.

"Gosh, Stefia," I said, again. "I'm really, really sorry…"

"Yeah, I'm sure," she said with a fake smile. "Well played, Raynee. Well played."

"Too afraid to come over to our badass bar?" I said. "Can't even take a shot with us?"

Stefia glared at me.

"Oh, that's right," I continued, talking to the party goers who had gathered around me. "Stefia's too good for us. She's too good to be in a high school play. Why are you even at this party, Stefia? Why don't you go hang out with your adult friends?"

Stefia didn't say anything. She just let her eyes burn into the flesh of my face. Then she turned to walk away.

But I wouldn't stop.

"Stefia!" I screamed at her. "Why are you here! You're too good for us, remember? You're too good to be badass!"

I turned to my friends who all held up their shot glasses in a sort of victory cheer. I'd told off Princess Stefia.

"Badass?" Stefia said quietly, as she slowly turned around. "Is that what you think this is?"

She made a circle in front of her with her finger, indicating the people standing around us. And like always, the room got quiet. That always happened when Stefia spoke. It was as if the sound waves from her voice infected anyone within range with a sort of magic dust and they couldn't *not* listen.

"Shut up, Stefia. I don't even want to hear you. Just shut up..."

"Badass?" she repeated, this time not any louder but far more intense.

"Are you deaf?" I asked. "Yeah, that's what I said. Badass."

"You think badass is sitting at a party doing some shots?" she said.

I shoved my shot glass at her face.

"Ooo," she said dryly. "Shots at a party. That's pretty crazy."

And I don't know what it was, but something inside told me I was about to see Stefia crack. From a stupid comment about taking a shot of birthday cake flavored vodka. And I couldn't resist. I had to keep going. I had to keep pushing.

"Come on, Stefia," I said, soothingly. "Let's be renegades together. Let's be rebels. Take a shot with me. You know all the guys here would probably cream in their pants if they saw good little Stefia take a shot. Shit, maybe some of the girls, too..."

"Renegade?" she repeated, adding a smirk of sarcasm. "Yeah, Raynee. You're a total renegade. I mean, gosh, this is just an insane amount of rule breaking..."

"Wait," I mocked. "You're right. Stupid shots at a high school party are lame. So very beneath you. What should we be doing, Stefia? What would make our party worth it for you?"

"You don't get it," she said. "You think you're doing something amazing by drinking at a party? Breaking rules about no drinking? What are you trying to prove, anyway?"

"Should we get out the harder stuff?" I threatened.

"Give me a break..."

"Because we can," I said, without skipping a beat. "It's here. If you really want to be badass."

"What harder stuff are you referring to? I mean, are you thinking pot is going to elevate you to stardom...or are you going to try meth or heroin or what? I mean, what are you talking about?" Her voice was getting louder and more intense. "If you're going to argue this with me, stop talking in riddles."

A bigger crowd had gathered to see what was going on. The murmurs through the people had changed from an excited *oh my god, Stefia is here* to *holy shit, something is going to happen...*

"Maybe she could step into the rainbow room," Jimmy offered from behind me, practically drooling at Stefia as he spoke to her. "Ever been to a rainbow party, Stefia baby? I know I'd like to slap some lipstick on you and see how..."

"How what? How...good I am on my knees?" Stefia finished.

I heard someone gasp. Someone actually gasped behind me. No one ever thought Princess Stefia would have a clue what a rainbow party was, let alone say something about being good on her knees.

Wait. She had to be pretending. She was playing along. She was acting. Yes, of course. It was classic Stefia, the actress.

"Good on your knees?" I laughed. "I bet the director of the next show at the Crystal Plains Theater will know how good you are on your knees."

Ah. Fighting words.

"What's that supposed to mean?" Stefia asked.

"Give me a break," I said, my courage bolstered by the last shot I'd taken. "Everyone knows how you get the roles at Crystal Plains."

"Really? And how is that?" Stefia egged me on.

"Hey, Stefia," I mocked. "Come here, you've got a little something on your chin, let me wipe that off..."

"For real, Raynee?" she said. "What makes you think I have to..."

"Drop the innocent act, bitch," I said, rolling my eyes. "It doesn't work for you. Just like most of the roles you get. They don't really work for you. But I guess when you're fucking the director, you end up with whatever role you want."

"Fuck you," Stefia said.

"I'm flattered," I mocked, "but as far as I can tell, you and I getting together isn't in your next script."

"Fuck you!"

And that's when it happened.

Snap.

Crackle

Pop.

Stefia flew at me, arms reaching, fingers spiked out like claws. She clutched at my neck and kept pushing on my throat until she'd knocked me through the crowd that had gathered and pinned me against a closet door.

I knew she was mad. But I had no clue how strong she actually was. At first, I thought she'd crack but it would be no big deal to me. I thought she'd pin me to the wall, it would be a good show, people would be shocked, I'd push her off…and then it would over.

But she wouldn't let up. And she was way stronger than anyone would have guessed.

"Stefia…stop…" I gasped, trying to peel her fingers off my neck.

Why wasn't anyone stopping her? Why wasn't anyone pulling her off me? Why were they all just standing there watching?

"Stefia, I can't breathe…"

"I have never slept with any director of any show!" she said, eyes fixed and steely.

"Okay, Stefia…I can't…"

"Never!" She pushed harder at my neck and I could swear I heard something crack. "Do you hear me?"

"Stefia, stop…" I was starting to black out. I was starting to…

Stefia released her grip and I slid to the floor, gagging for air. She just stood there staring at me.

And everyone else stared at Stefia.

"You don't know me," she said. "You don't know one fucking thing about me."

She turned to walk away but I coughed out more words.

"That's because you're an act," I spat, rubbing at my neck. "Every single thing about you is an act. How are we supposed to know who the fuck you really are?"

Stefia turned back to glare at me, her eyes digging into mine, blazing their way through the flesh of my face. I felt like a suffocating pile of ashes.

Stop looking at me, Stefia.

Stop looking at me.

She wouldn't stop looking at me, so I closed my eyes. And then my lips spread into a warm and twisty smile.

I'd seen Princess Stefia crack.

**

People think I'm nuts for going to her funeral. People think I shouldn't be here because they know we didn't get along. At all. But even after that night at the party when she sent me collapsing into a heap on the floor, I've always kept in the back of my mind the belief that if Stefia could have been more honest, she and I would have been much better friends. Because I totally get being kissed by an older man who shouldn't be kissing you.

We could have been friends. Or at least we could have helped each other out.

See, Stefia wasn't just an actress on stage, she was an actress in every aspect of her life. But it doesn't matter now. You see, there's no pretending anymore. Show is over.

Everybody go home.

-Elliot-

Elliot! Run with me!

I can still see her, nine-years-old, racing down the dark driveway with a lit sparkler in both hands. It was almost midnight and she was still in her swimsuit and a pair of pink denim shorts.

I remember that 4th of July. Our parents had spent the afternoon laughing, eating, and drinking around the campfire. By the time the sun went down, they were only giving us kids half a glance worth of attention.

Elliot! Come on!

Looking back to even my earliest memories, there are always pieces of Stefia that flit across my mind. Her parents and my parents were best friends—our mothers delivered us only two weeks apart—so she and I spent our childhood together. I imagine we started out toddling around in the front yard of one house or the other while our mothers sipped cocktails and complained about the woes of parenthood. Then we grew up and in elementary school attacked the county fair, sped bikes down the alleys in town, waded out way too far in the river, and spent hours slipping down the twisty slide on my tree fort. Such was life when your parents were always together and you looked for ways to waste the day.

We were happily inseparable.

Elliot! Come in, the water is so warm!

I taught her how to bait a hook. She taught me how to skip a rock even if it wasn't flat on one side.

No, Elliot. Hold it like this. Now snap your wrist...

I guess you could say she was like the sister I never had. Stefia's own sister, Gabriella, was kind of a princess and Naomi spent most of her time playing Pokémon with my brothers Mitch and Michael. But Stefia and I, man...we were going to conquer the world.

Bring that board over here. It will work better for the front of the raft...

I won't lie. I kind of liked pretending she was my sister. Well, at least in the beginning.

**

One night, as I was distracted by what video games to add to the wish list for my upcoming birthday, my mom cleared her throat halfway through dinner and announced that Stefia's parents had split up. Then, without another thought, she asked me to pass the milk.

Split up?

Stefia's parents?

"You're kidding, right?" I asked. "Like...the Stefia we just went to the Granite Ledge parade with last week?"

"Son," dad said, scooping a second helping of macaroni and cheese onto his plate, "do you know any other Stefia?"

I set my fork down and stared at the globs of cheesy noodles on my plate. Part of me said the news didn't matter. Like, why should I care? People split up all the time.

But a bigger part of me knew it did matter.

"Like...they are getting a divorce?"

"Yes. I believe so," my mother said, pouring herself a glass of milk and then refilling mine. "I'm sorry."

It seemed to me that my parents were oddly detached from the situation. It was almost as if the fact their best friends had split up would force them turn inwards and reflect on the state of their own marriage, chalking up how we are not like them in one column and how we are more similar to them than we'd like to admit in another. They didn't want to make those lists, and so they just ignored the situation all together.

I put my napkin on the table, pushed my chair away, and stood up.

"I think I'm done eating."

It really shouldn't have mattered to me. It's not like they were my parents.

"Elliot," my dad said. "Look, it's gonna be okay…"

I held my hand up to signal he should stop talking.

He did.

"I'm sorry," I said. "I just…I need to go for a walk."

**

I found Stefia alone at the park on a swing. She was barefoot, twisting her big toe into the trench underneath the swing made by years' worth of kids dragging their feet to slow themselves down.

I took a seat in the swing next to her, smirking to myself because at almost fourteen and pushing five foot nine, I was sort of like the giant in *Gulliver's Travels*. My butt barely fit in the swing and the seat was too low, which made my knees sit parallel with my shoulders. She didn't say anything, just stared at the hole her big toe was making.

The park was surrounded by spindly pine trees that rose around us like sharpened pencils poking at the sky. Kids had made hiding places at the bottoms of the trees, using the heavy, low branches as shelter during their games of Ghosts in the Graveyard or Bloody Mary.

After a while, Stefia looked up from her swing at me with a wobbly smile—mostly out of obligation, I think.

"I'm assuming since you're sitting here and haven't said anything," she started, "that it's because you heard the news and you don't know what to say."

"That would be a correct assumption," I said.

Two kids bolted from under the pine trees and zig-zagged across the short clipped grass in an impromptu game of tag. Their tennis shoes stomped at the ground and their giggles floated on the breeze.

Stefia and I had done that so many times.

"You really don't have to say anything. It's okay."

"Maybe," I started thoughtfully, "I should have googled 'the right thing to say when your friends' parents split' before I came over here."

"Nah," she said, picking up her feet and letting the swing move. "Google probably would have been wrong."

"Google is never wrong," I said. "Ever."

I picked up my feet and tried to swing but since I was too tall and too heavy, I didn't even move. Stefia laughed.

"Hey," I said.

"What?"

"I'm sorry."

"For what?"

"Your parents. Them breaking up. The divorce…or whatever. I'm sorry."

"You don't have to be sorry," she said, pumping her legs and swinging higher. "It wasn't your fault."

"I know…but…"

"Wait," she cut me off. "I think you actually *did* Google to find out the correct response, and *I'm sorry* is what Google said."

I laughed.

"Google is totally lame," she said. "Totally. It doesn't even make sense. Why does someone say they are sorry for something they didn't have anything to do with? You can't apologize for something that isn't your fault."

"Hey, we could Google why people say sorry…"

"We could."

She dragged her feet to stop her swing, kicking up sand and covering her purple toenails with a layer of dust.

"Listen," I said, not looking at her. "I don't want to get weird or anything, but you know...if you ever want to talk, and your girl friends are all busy or something..."

"Elliot?"

"What?

"I thought you didn't want to make this weird..."

"Oh. Was it weird?"

She smirked.

"A little."

"Well, I just...you know, wanted you to know if you ever..."

"I get it, Elliot. Thanks."

She grabbed on to the chains and lifted herself from the swing. She walked away from me, slowly, kicking at the sand and tiny pebbles that settled around the playground equipment.

"Where you going?" I asked.

"I'm gonna go to the pine trees," she said. "I think I'm just gonna hide out for a while. Know what I mean?"

"Sure."

She turned and walked towards the tree line that seemed to stand as a picture frame around the entire park. She headed for the north corner, the thickest and darkest part of the pine trees.

"Hey!" I called to her.

"What?" she answered without turning around.

"You...want some company?"

She stopped walking. She looked up at the sky and I could see her shoulders rise and then fall in what must have been a huge sigh.

She didn't answer me but she also didn't start walking so I got out of the stupid miniature swing I was still sitting in and jogged up behind her.

"Hey. I asked if you wanted some company."

I put my hand on her shoulder and she turned around to look at me.

She was crying.

"Oh, god. Stefia, I'm sorry..."

I didn't know what I was supposed to do. I couldn't remember a time in my life that didn't include Stefia, and yet I couldn't remember a time she'd ever cried in front of me.

"Listen," I said. "It's going to be okay… it's going to be fine…"

"Shut up," she said. "Don't say anything."

"Okay."

"Like, anything. Just don't talk."

"Okay."

She glared at me.

"Sorry," I said.

"Just come sit with me in the trees."

"What?"

"Just come sit with me," she said slowly, "and don't talk."

I almost said okay, but then I remembered, and I just nodded.

She sniffled and fixed her eyes on me. Then she turned back towards the forest and I followed her into the cover of pine trees.

I wish I could look back on that day and remember it as being full of comfort. I wish I could say that it was the day I knew I'd had some part in helping Stefia move forward, but that's really not the case.

You see, I look at that day as the beginning of the end.

**

At first when I heard someone was opening a theater just outside Granite Ledge, I thought it was a joke. Who in the world would open a theater in a community made of drunks and farmers? Who is going to pay money to watch people parade around on stage in costume?

And why in the world would Stefia want anything to do with it?

But that theater took off like no one would have ever imagined. Suddenly there was culture in Granite Ledge, propelled forward by a gussied up Stefia who paraded herself around and poured herself out to her pile of adoring fans.

The first play she was in, I thought okay, whatever. It's something for her to do. Something to distract her from the mess with her parents. But as time went on, it almost seemed as though the theater was a distraction from real life.

Or, from like…fishing with her friend.

Or hanging out at the park.

Or getting ice cream at Beidermanns.

Or just sitting around laughing about stupid cat videos on YouTube.

There was never any time for anything but the theater.

I mean, don't get me wrong. People thought she was amazing. She captivated the town in a string of performances that were worthy of a small town Tony. But when I watched her in a show, I just saw Stefia reading lines.

"Why do you care?" mom asked me one Sunday morning. We sat at the table eating pancakes before we all went fishing at Red Lake.

"Because it seems like she's pretending."

"Well, it is acting."

"That's not what I mean," I said, and forked three pancakes off the platter in the center of the table.

Why didn't anyone understand what I was saying?

By the third show, over a year from when we hid out in the pine trees, she was a completely different person.

"It's like now she's a whole other story," I complained to my dad one evening while watching my youngest brother get pummeled in his homecoming game. "She's like a character from a book that she never would have thought of reading before."

"Son, if you haven't figured out by now that girls— women—are weird, then you're slower than I thought." He playfully punched at my shoulder and looked amused.

"I don't think this is just her being a weird girl."

"What do you mean?"

"I can't put my finger on it. She's not the Stefia I used to know."

"Makes sense," he said. "She's growing up. You're growing up. People change as they grow."

I shook my head.

"I just think there is something going on. She's just so...I don't know, antithetic."

"That's a five dollar word, son," he said, sipping from the straw in his soda. "You use those words around her? Maybe that's why she seems different. She doesn't understand what the hell you're saying..."

"Dad, stop. You know what I mean. She's like, night and day different. I can't even talk to her..."

"Then don't."

"What?"

He set his soda down, looked out onto the field for Mitch, and then popped his fist up in the air in some father-son moment of encouragement.

"Listen, son. If there's anything I've learned, it's that you can't change the mind of a person who doesn't want to be changed. She's going through some stuff right now, sure. But you can only do so much to help her. And then...well, you just..."

"Give up?"

"No, don't give up. Just, I don't know...keep an eye out for her, but don't get wrapped up in the mess. If she needs you, she knows where to find you. She'll come around."

**

I'd kinda forgotten about Stefia by the time our senior year started.

Okay, that's not the truth, but that's what I tried to convince myself and everyone else of. I failed miserably because, well, you know when you just miss someone and you just need to see them? I'd stop by Stefia's locker at school a couple times a month to make small talk. I'd show up at the coffee shop every so often and order a latte just to see how she was. She was always distant; some stiff and unconcerned version of Stefia that Stefia would have hated if she'd seen it in the mirror.

Shortly after our senior year began, my mom announced she'd been diagnosed with a *touch* of cancer. The doctors said things like *found it early* and *treatable* and *operation* and *full recovery* but my brain spun in dramatic circles around the less positive and completely possible outcome. And as I contemplated life without my mother, I knew there was only one person I could talk to who would even remotely understand life without a mother, and suddenly I needed to talk to Stefia. I asked around school the next day and found out she'd be at theater that night for final dress rehearsal.

I knew dress rehearsals went late, but I was a patient person. I casually strolled through her neighborhood about 11 pm, listening to the late night noises of small town Minnesota, waiting for her to get home so I could talk about my mom.

"Why don't you just text her?" Mitch had asked me earlier that evening.

"She never answers when I do."

"And you haven't taken that as a sign yet?"

"Shut up."

"Listen," Mitch said. "I get it. You used to hang out and play pirates and build forts, but we aren't kids anymore. How long are you going to waste your time with her?"

I had shaken my head when he said that, and I shook my head again as I walked to get rid of the conversation. I was not wasting my time. Something in my gut told me so.

An old car rolled quietly down the road and pulled into the driveway directly across from Stefia's house. It pulled under the security light of the garage, revealing a nice old Cutlass from the early 70s. Olive green or maybe some weird greenish yellow, it was hard to tell in the fluorescent of the bulb on the garage.

And then I saw Stefia get out of the passenger side of the car. But she didn't walk across the street to her own house. She shut her car door, giggled something I couldn't quite hear, and followed the driver to the front door of the house.

The driver fumbled in his pocket for something, presumably keys to unlock the door, which seemed to take much longer than it should have.

As I watched them, something just seemed...off. Not right.

It's just that she was standing so close to him, you know? The boundaries that should have been there were sketchy. That bubble of personal space that everyone has...was completely missing from the both of them.

He finally got the door open and made a sweeping gesture in front of him to signify he was a gentleman and she should go first. She walked ahead of him and I could have sworn I saw his hand brush her ass as she passed.

But it couldn't be. Because…

Let's get one thing straight. I knew that Stefia wasn't into me. I wasn't into her like that, either. Honestly. So what I felt that night wasn't jealousy over her losing her personal bubble of space with some guy. No. It was disgust— because the guy she'd lost her personal space with looked old enough to be her father.

Suddenly, I had an overwhelming urge. I needed to follow her.

Before I knew it, I'd crept across the street, ducked behind the hedge that lined his driveway, and was sitting between his trashcan and a giant hose reel in front of his garage. I couldn't believe I was going to spy on her. What if she found out? And what was I thinking I would find, anyway?

I was hoping I didn't find anything. I was hoping I was wrong.

It took me a full five minutes to get the courage to stand up from my hiding spot. Then I slinked to a sidewalk between the house and garage, hoping there were no motion detector lights waiting to reveal my whereabouts. It took another three minutes for me to listen in an attempt to figure out where they were in the house. I only occasionally heard voices and couldn't make out any of the muffled words.

There was a window that would show what I believed to be the front room of the house, and I figured it would be a good place to start looking. I stretched my neck to try and peek between a slit in the blinds. I was just too short so I looked for something to stand on to look in. I found a couple loose paver bricks and quietly stacked them to make myself tall enough. I stood on the bricks, slowly moved my head to line up with the blinds and...

Oh. God.

Fuck.

I mean, Seriously. Fuck.

Now, I wasn't a hundred percent sure about what I saw on his red leather couch.

But I was sure enough.

My mouth watered with the acid of nausea and I heaved. I lost my footing on the stack of bricks, which caused them to topple over.

A dog barked from inside the house.

I ran.

**

Even though it was 1:15 in the morning, I made up my mind that I would wait for her. And because the bottom of a tree makes a pretty good place to hide, I decided to camp out under the giant tree in her yard while I watched for her to return home. Eventually, she would have to come back.

At 2 am, she snuck her way into her driveway. I waited until her bare feet hit the grass.

"Hey," I said, from where I sat.

She jumped and then clutched her hand to her chest, gasping. She looked towards the tree, barely able to see me except for the three quarter moon.

"Jesus Christ," she said. "You scared me."

She took a few more deep breaths.

"Elliot, what are you doing here?"

"Looking for you."

I looked across the street to the house she'd just come from. The lights were all dark now, including the light that had illuminated the front porch.

I stared at that house. And when she realized I was hyper-focused on his front door, she knew.

She knew I'd seen I'd seen something.

"How long have you been here?"

"Long enough."

She adjusted her bag on her shoulder and then pulled at a rubber band around her wrist.

"Look. Elliot. I know it probably looks like something is going on…"

"You're right. It does."

"But…it's not what you think."

Then she fixed the most charming and plastic smile on her lips, almost like she was posing for a camera. Like, if she said it as convincingly as possible, then I should believe whatever came out of her mouth. The only problem was that she wasn't convincing. At all.

"Who lives there?" I asked, pointing across the road.

"His name is Niles."

"What were you doing?"

"Are you spying on me?"

"No. What were you doing?"

"What are you…my father?"

"I'm only asking because…"

"Maybe you shouldn't worry about it, okay?"

She jumped down my throat just a little too quickly for me to believe that I shouldn't worry about it.

"It's theater stuff," she said, finally.

"He's in the theater?"

"He owns the theater," she said, matter-of-factly. "We were practicing for a scene."

"Stefia, from what I saw, that guy is old enough to be your dad. Shit, I bet he's older than your dad."

"We were just practicing a scene," she repeated calmly.

"Why do you need to practice anything?" I asked. "You should have everything down pat by now seeing as how tonight was your final dress rehearsal."

"How would you even know that? You don't give a shit about the theater."

"I asked around. I found out where you were."

"Are you stalking me?" She adjusted her bag on her shoulder and turned away from me, pawing her hand through her hair.

"I'm not stalking you. I'm just worried about you."

"It's two in the morning!" she said. "Why are you out wondering what I'm doing?"

"Why are you out so I have to wonder?"

"Great, just great!" she said, and she spun her body around to spit more words at me. "I totally did not expect this from you, Elliot…"

"Expect what?"

"You're jealous. Jesus Christ, Elliot, you're just like every other person in this town with a dick."

"What's that supposed to mean?"

"You're mad if you're not the one who gets to be with me."

"Be with you?" I yelled. "Stefia, get over yourself! Not everyone in this town wants to sleep with you…"

"Oh yeah? Name one."

"Me."

"Bullshit."

"Stefia, it is possible to care about what happens to you and not want to see you naked."

"I beg to differ."

"Me? Elliot? Who has known you since forever?" I yelled. "How can you even think I would want to…I mean, Christ. What the hell is wrong with you?"

"How about you not waste your time wondering…"

 "Listen, I don't know if you've punched up the drama because you're part of the theater or what, but it's annoying. It's stupid. And it's not you, Stefia. I know you. I've always known you."

"Shut up, Elliot," she said. "I don't want to hear it. How about you go find something else to do? Go get drunk. Go find a girlfriend. I don't care what you do, but stop worrying about me."

She turned from me.

"Don't walk away…"I said, and grabbed her arm to spin her back around.

"Let me go."

"No, Stefia. Don't walk away from me." I grabbed her other wrist and held her in front of me.

"I said let me go!"

She tried to pull away but I held tight.

"God damn it, let me go!" she screamed, pulling at her arms to free them. She raised her boot to kick me but I twisted my body and her boot stuck hard, right in my thigh. I let go of her and squeezed at my leg, trying to rub out the sharp ache her boot had planted where it landed.

"Stay away from me!" she hissed. "I mean it."

Her porch light snapped on suddenly and I could see Naomi peek her head out from behind the curtain in the front window. Stefia picked up her bag and spun herself to head to the house.

"Stefia…" I started.

"I mean it, Elliot," she said, barely above a whisper. "Leave me alone. I have nothing to say to you."

She walked in the house and turned off the porch light. I stood on the sidewalk, still rubbing at my leg. I stared at her front door. God, I wanted to bust down that door and follow her in, shake her until she made sense. But I was taken over by my dad's cautionary recommendation to not get caught up in the mess.

And Stefia was definitely a mess.

**

Three days later, I heard it.

"Bro! You are a total dog!"

We were in the locker room after running the track and Ben smacked me way too hard on the shoulder.

"Um, what?" I said, sitting on a bench between the rows of lockers and pulling my shirt off over my head.

"Totally tried to score with Stefia?"

I raised an eyebrow.

"Um…no, I didn't."

"That's the talk all over school," Ben said.

"It is? What are they saying?"

He looked at me, not buying my disbelief.

"El-Man, give it up. You tried to score with her and…"

"No," I said, shaking my head. "No, I didn't…"

"She pushed you off and you followed her to her house and then had a big fight with her right on the sidewalk."

"Oh, my god. That's totally not what happened," I said, thinking back on how our conversation three nights earlier might have sounded to anyone within earshot. "Not even close. I mean, we did argue about some stuff but someone must have heard it and assumed…"

"So what really happened," Ben said. "You did score with her?"

"Shut-up! Nothing like that even happened. I wouldn't want anything like that to happen. It would be like…screwing my sister."

"So…it's a rumor?"

"Why is it so hard to believe it's a rumor?" I said. "Shit, Ben, why would I want to sleep with someone I've known since she was like…born?"

"Um, because that girl is fucking hot."

The hairs on the back of my neck pricked up and something told me Ben was going to take it too far.

"Don't talk about her like that," I said.

"What…are you like, her protector or something?"

"What's it to you?"

"Come on," he said and laughed. "Admit it. She's like a piece of candy you'd like to play with in your mouth."

"I said don't talk about her like that…"

I stood up, still in my running shorts. I was a whole head taller than him, but he didn't back down. He adjusted his posture to look bigger but still didn't even come close to being my size.

"Like what? Is there something wrong with pointing out she's a sweet piece of ass and there isn't one guy in this school who wouldn't like two minutes alone with her?"

"Wow, two minutes. That's impressive, you fucking prick."

"Two minutes is all it would take…"

And that's when I fixed my wild and stupid eyes on him, and barreled my fists into his chest. His stomach. His head. He held his arms up to block me but I couldn't stop punching him. I couldn't stop until he shut up. My fists connected over and over again with his skin, the flesh on his face splitting as I pounded it open. He collapsed in a rigid heap to the floor, arms wrapped around his head in a shell of protection.

Two guys jumped in to pull me off of him. They held me back, both of them restraining an arm. That's when I saw blood all over the white tile floor—Ben's, not mine.

Ben removed his arms from covering his head and grabbed at the front of his face, blood gushing from his nose and lip. His ear was cut, his cheek was sliced.

"You broke my fucking nose!"

"Who did you hear the rumor from!" I screamed. The two guys on either side of me pulled back harder, one's fingers gouging into my bicep.

"It's not a fucking rumor," he said, spitting blood on the floor.

"How the hell would you know?"

He wiped blood across his chin with the back of his hand and looked up to meet my eyes.

"Because," he said, "I heard it from Stefia."

**

I waited in the back lot of the Crystal Plains Theater, knowing at any minute the stage door would open and Stefia would bounce out. The show had been done for forty-five minutes. She had to be coming out soon. My hands were sweating. I paced like a caged animal. I was almost done with my third cigarette, and I didn't even smoke.

"Hey!" I called to her when the door finally opened. She walked out with a fellow actress, both of them laughing and smiling and jingling their keys. I stood only fifteen feet from the stage door, but she acted like she didn't know where the voice had come from. So I walked right up to her.

"I'm going to cut right to the point," I said, serious and biting. I sucked my last drag off the cigarette and looked at her. "You need to explain something to me."

Her cast mate shot a worried look, like I was some psycho there to rip her apart, but Stefia waved her off with a roll of her eyes. The girl hit the button on her key fob to unlock her door. She gave one more look at Stefia, then got in her car.

We didn't talk until the car was gone.

"Classy," she started, "showing up here at the theater to chew me out."

"Far classier than you," I said, tossing my cigarette butt on the ground and smashing it with the toe of my boot. "Telling people I tried to…"

"Stop being so dramatic," she interrupted. "People start rumors all the time."

"You're not even going to deny it?" I practically choked.

"Would it be easier for you if I did?"

I kicked at the ground and spattered rocks ahead of me.

"Could we maybe not talk like this is an unsolved mystery where I need to decode all your answers into an actual dialogue?"

"I'm not trying to be difficult," she said, with a strange calmness. "Sometimes the fatal flaw in a conversation is that the two people talking view the world in different ways."

"You're not that different from me," I said. "Stop trying to drive a wedge between us that doesn't belong there."

"How do you know what belongs there? Who do you think you are? God, himself? Christ, Elliot, just..."

"Stefia, don't fuck this up. You're going to screw up your life and push away everyone who cares about you..."

"You act like I don't know what I'm doing."

"I don't think you do."

She smirked.

"I know exactly what I'm doing."

"Trying to push me away? Trying to make me hate you?"

"This is not about that," she answered. "This is about protection."

"Who the fuck are you trying to protect?"

"I can tell you who it isn't."

I waited for it, knowing she was finally going to reveal me as the person she could care less about. The person who wasn't worth her time. The person she could just forget even existed.

"Okay, then. Who?" I taunted. "Tell me what pathetic soul creeps around this earth and doesn't deserve to be protected from whatever chaos it is that you've tripped upon."

She looked straight into my eyes.

"Me."

My mouth was dry and I tried to speak but nothing came out.

"Don't you get it, Elliot?" she said. "I'm trying to protect you."

"That makes no fucking sense!" I yelled.

"Why not? Elliot, please. You're like a brother to me. I don't want you to get hurt…"

"Jesus Christ, Stefia," I said, kicking at the ground. "I saw you with Niles. I saw what happened! And you say you're protecting me from you?"

"I can't explain it to you," she said, her voice starting to shake. "Just please believe me that I know what I'm doing…

"I can't believe I got sucked into this mess," I said, raking my hands through my hair. "I mean, do you think he's in love with you? For fuck's sake, Stefia, don't you get it?"

"Get what?"

"He's using you!" I screamed, my voice cracking with anger.

A tear spilled from the corner of her eye and her lip quivered.

"Yeah. Well, maybe I'm using him, too."

My stare of incredulity morphed into one of repulsion.

"My god," I said. "You know what you are?"

"What? I'm dying to know," she said, sniffling. "Please tell me what you think, oh great and mighty Elliot."

"You're a whore, Stefia. Plain and simple. You're a fucking whore."

She exploded, lighting up like a firecracker and attacking with everything she had. Her clenched fist cracked at my jaw with such force that after the connection, the leftover momentum propelled her right to the ground. I immediately grabbed my jaw, kneading the bone with my thumb, and stared in disbelief.

She had hit me. She had actually fucking hit me.

She lay on the ground, holding herself up on her side with one arm. She looked up and nervously studied my face, bracing herself for whatever I would bring next.

"You know what, Stefia?" I said, my voice calm and calculated. "Fuck you. Fuck Niles. Fuck this theater. I have *always* been there for you."

"Elliot..."

"No. Shut up, Stefia. Now if you want my help, *you* come find *me*."

I turned and walked to my car, not waiting to hear anymore of her excuses or explanations. I yanked open the car door, threw myself inside, and slammed it so hard it threatened to fall off its hinges. Twisting the key into the ignition, I shoved the car in gear before I even heard the engine rev. I gunned it and sent a spray of gravel behind me, dust settling on Stefia who did nothing but lie on the ground and watch me speed away.

I didn't know it then, but that night was the end of the end.

**

My father parked the car in the church lot. I had opted to ride with my parents. Why, I'm not sure. Power in numbers, or something like that.

My mom, ever fearful of the media, ditched the car immediately and ducked into the church. I could have cared

251

less who was watching and decided I would sit in the car until I was good and ready to do otherwise.

My dad stayed in the front seat.

"We can sit in here as long as you'd like," he said. "No rush."

We stayed in the car with the engine idling. I thought about telling him to turn the car off; that even though we were parked in a lot bordered by snow and it was only twenty degrees, there was no way I was going to get cold. But I didn't. Whether the car was on or off made no difference to anything.

"Dad?"

"Yes, son?"

Our eyes met momentarily in the rearview mirror. I looked away.

"You told me something once," I said. "Something I never forgot."

I could tell he was still looking at me in the mirror but I couldn't meet his eyes. I stared out the window at the pathetic reporters and their equipment. I hoped they all froze.

"What is it, son?"

"Well, you told me that Stefia knew where I lived, and that if she needed me, she knew where to find me. You said she'd come around. "

I saw my father shift uncomfortably in his seat.

"Dad, she never came and found me."

I waited a minute for him to respond but the air inside the car had grown eerily thick, like a bubble, pressing at the windows, that wouldn't break.

"Am I supposed to assume now that she really didn't need me?"

I looked down at my jet black suit pants. I picked at an imaginary stray thread to keep from completely losing the flood of tears I was holding back.

"Son," he finally spoke, blowing out a heavy sigh. He curled his fingers slowly around the steering wheel like he was imagining he could drive himself right out of the conversation.

"I mean, I waited, dad. Just like you said. I waited for her to come find me. Because I really thought she was going to."

I looked up to the rearview mirror again, but dad wasn't looking this time. His eyes were pointed out the window in the direction of the cameras and press, but I knew he didn't see any of it.

"I believed that she was going to come. Know why, dad? Because I believed you."

A gray Kia pulled up next to us and parked. Two men and a woman got out. I had no idea who they were. The woman pulled her black full length dress coat around her tighter, and one of the men put his arm around her shoulder. The three of them walked stoically into the church together. I wondered who they were. I wondered how they knew Stefia. I wondered…well, I wondered a lot of stuff.

I guess that had always been my problem.

"Son, I'm sorry," he finally said.

"You want to know the worst part? The worst part is that now I'm never going to know if she needed me or not."

"I know this hurts, Elliot."

"Why her, dad?"

And suddenly there was something so real about her being dead. Something so hard to swallow about the not knowing if where we'd stood was real or if her stone-faced carelessness was all an act. I tried to breathe in and choked on a whole glut of tears I'd held back. And then they wouldn't stop, a huge ugly sobbing flood slopping down my face.

"Fuck!" I screamed, slamming my fists down into the back of the seat. "I fucking hate this!"

I bawled, almost suffocating on everything that was coming up and out of me.

"Why her, dad? Answer me!"

I looked into the rearview mirror and met dad's eyes again.

"Elliot," he said. "I don't know."

"What do you mean, you don't know?"

"I mean that sometimes we just don't know. Sometimes we can't know."

Dad looked away from the mirror, his voice constricting, and I knew he was going to cry.

"Sometimes, Elliot....sometimes we're not supposed to know."

I stared straight ahead at the flat brick wall of the church. I couldn't look at him. Because as much as I hated to admit it, I knew he was right.

-Pastor Walter-

I placed my hand on the top of the black matte frame that hung on my wall, remembering how Stefia was so excited to be in that first show four years ago. I remembered how she seemed to come alive on opening night, uncovering a side of herself that no one knew she hid beneath her skin. She was electric; a perfect sphere of sparks, blazing a streak as far into her future as one dared to imagine.

I pulled the frame off the wall and laid it face down on my desk.

I couldn't look at that picture anymore.

Outside my window, the media perched like blood-thirsty cannibals across the road, ready to devour anyone willing to speak on camera. They hungered for the next quote. The next clip.

Signs had been placed in front of the church informing the press they were not to set foot on church property. You wouldn't think you'd have to say that to another human being. You wouldn't think you'd have to tell someone that our town is in mourning and we want to be left alone. I wished I could hang a black veil over the entire community, wrapping us back in the bubble of anonymity we'd enjoyed before the whole mess began.

Randall, our police chief, had stood in the doorway of my office three days ago after someone leaked details about the funeral to the press. He said, "Walter, we're going to need security for this funeral. It's going to be a mess."

"Security at a funeral?" It was a new one for me.

He leaned against the doorframe and rubbed his forehead like he was trying to rub the whole thing away.

"Yeah," he said. "This funeral...it's just going to be a nightmare."

"The whole damn thing is a nightmare. The funeral is just a small part."

"Yeah," he said, popping four ibuprofen in his mouth and swallowing them without water. He'd been chief for twenty-five years, longer than I'd been a pastor, and I know he'd never seen anything like this in Granite Ledge.

None of us had.

**

Generally, I don't mind funerals. I don't have a problem officiating them. Funerals are supposed to be a celebration of life. Two months ago, Edith Fletcher passed away. She had spent her entire ninety-five years of life as a member of the church and we were so sad to lose her here on earth. No more almond cakes. No more lap quilts. And no more hearing her joyfully belt out *Blessed Assurance*, slightly off key.

But she had lived almost a century. She died peacefully in her sleep. She'd lived her life, fulfilled her dreams, marked everything off her bucket list. She had lived happy, she died happy, and her funeral was, in the truest sense of the word, a celebration of that long and full life.

But Stefia's funeral is not.

I want it to be. I should be able to walk to the pulpit with marked solemnity but effective hope and speak comforting words about heaven. I should be able to smile warmly at the family and friends who gather in her honor.

I should be able to do that.

But I don't think I can.

**

One month ago, Stefia had quietly knocked on my office door. She came in, sat down silently across from me and set her hands in her lap. My cluttered desk separated us but I could tell she was nervous.

It was uncharacteristic for Stefia.

Not once in the fourteen years she'd attended my church had she ever asked if we could talk privately. I wasn't sure what to expect, but ran through several scenarios in my head, guessing at the path of the upcoming meeting. One thing I assumed was that the conversation would flow freely. Everyone knew Stefia could sell ice to an Eskimo or make a conversation with a brick wall seem exciting, so it didn't seem like a Tuesday morning conference in my office would be any trouble at all.

But sitting across from me in the crimson padded chair, Stefia was quiet. Too quiet to be the Stefia I'd watched grow up in church.

"Can I get you something?" I asked. "A water? Some coffee?"

She shook her head and absent mindedly rubbed at her thighs, so I sat down in my office chair. I rested my elbows on the desk and folded my hands under my chin. Our eyes met momentarily but she looked away, saying nothing.

"You wanted to talk about something?" I prodded gently.

"Yes," she cleared her throat. "I do."

"Well, what a coincidence." I smiled. "That's what I'm here for."

She took a deep breath in.

"Pastor?"

I waited, thinking she would continue, but she didn't. She just took another deep breath and then smiled weakly.

As I watched her eyes move about the room, stopping to read book titles on my shelf and identify people in pictures on my wall, I couldn't help but notice how beat down and drained she looked.

"You have a picture of me here?" she asked, interrupting my thoughts of concern. She got up from the chair and walked over to the frame that encased a memory of her on my wall.

"I have many pictures of members of the congregation in my office."

Her eyes drifted across the many photographs, souvenirs of my twenty years as a pastor at First Light Lutheran. Arms around the shoulders of members of my congregation made up the bulk of them. So many photos at so many functions. The Santa Lucia Festival. Lenten soup suppers. The outdoor bluegrass concert to raise money for the church addition.

"But this one," she said, pointing to the picture of her, "is different. My picture isn't from anything that happened at church."

"You're right," I said, rising. "Stefia, you must realize that I don't spend my entire life in church."

"I know, but this picture is of..."

"Your first play," I finished, with a reminiscing smile. "Yes. We were all so proud of you...our little Stefia, shining like the brightest star up there on that big stage."

She squinted at the picture like she didn't know what it was, and then shook her head ever so slightly.

"But why not a picture of me teaching Sunday school?" she argued. "Or singing with the choir? Or serving a soup supper?"

"Oh, I have pictures of you doing all those wonderful things, too. I guess I've just grown accustomed to looking at this one from my desk."

I expected even a half smile, but nothing came.

"Stefia, is something troubling you?"

She walked from picture to picture, running her fingers over the multicolored frames. Then she opened her mouth to speak, but was so quiet it almost seemed as though she was whispering to the people staring back at her from the wall.

"I need to know that I matter."

"What?"

"That's all I need," she said, turning around to look at me squarely. "I need to know that I matter. Stefia Lenae Krist. I need to know that she matters to the world."

"Oh, dear Stefia." I walked around the front of my desk and put my hand on her shoulder. "You, of all people, should know that you matter."

"Why?" She turned and my hand dropped from where it had rested. "What does that even mean? *You of all people should know...*"

Her eyes showed she was irked, bothered by something I'd insinuated. She deflated back into her chair, frustration seeming to weigh her down.

"Stefia, let's be serious," I said. I moved back to the desk, sat down in my chair, and sighed. I felt we were destined for a game of cat and mouse. Hide and seek. I would chase her around the room, hoping for answers she would only give in riddles. "How in the world could you believe that you don't matter?"

"Give me a reason that I should assume I do."

Riddles and side steps. Impossibilities to decode. Questions with responses that meant something entirely different.

I reached across the desk and took Stefia's hands in mine.

"Stefia, listen to me. You are a valuable person. You are a beautiful and talented young woman who…"

"I'm pregnant."

Her fleshy words slopped ungraciously over the edge of her lips, like muck over a beautiful waterfall. They filled up my ears until they rang with disbelief.

 "Did you hear me, Pastor? Pregnant. I'm *pregnant*."

"Stefia, I…"

"You don't know what to say, right?"

Autopilot helped me to squeeze Stefia's hands with a polite smile. Then I let go and leaned back in my chair. I sighed. It was a sigh that seemed to take forever, and the time it took did not help me to come up with the right response to her news.

"Stefia…

My inept attempt at words of comfort spilled out in a string of stutters.

"I get it," she said. "Shocking, I know. Knocks me right down off that pedestal the whole town has me on."

"No," I said, emphatically. "It doesn't. This isn't about judgment, Stefia. I just…it's not what I was expecting you to come in here and talk to me about."

"Trust me," she said. "This wasn't something I planned. I should be worrying about lines on stage rather than how to break this news in real life."

The longer I stumbled over my response, the more the bubble of discomfort grew. It ballooned and threatened to pop.

Why won't the words come?

"So...the father," I began. "Is he in the picture?"

She nodded.

"Have you told him?"

She bit on her lip.

"I haven't told anyone yet. Well, except for you."

Did she see the look of surprise wash over my face? Why me? Stefia, with her multitude of friends, who got along with everyone...chose to give me first dibs on her news?

She looked down in her lap.

Why not her girl friends? Why not her sisters?

I swallowed hard.

"The first thing you asked me when you came here today," I said finally, "was about whether or not you matter. How can you think you don't matter, Stefia? Especially now, when you tell me you're going to have a baby..."

264

"I didn't say I was having a baby," she said, a solid stop on the last word. "I said I was pregnant."

Her words mashed through my head, swirling into the ugliest of messes.

"You're planning to have an abortion?"

"I didn't say that either."

Oh, god. The riddles. Why didn't she come out and say what she wanted?

"You're...here to get advice on what to do," I said.

"No, I'm here to find out if anyone can tell me if I really matter."

"I've already told you that you matter, Stefia. The whole town knows you matter. They don't generally place people who don't matter up on a pedestal."

"I didn't ask to be put on that pedestal."

She wanted me to drag it out of her.

I was determined to see inside her head.

"See, Stefia, that doesn't make sense to me. You want to know if you matter...but, if I'm reading you correctly, you're almost acting annoyed for the attention. I'm confused." Then I stopped. "I think you really came here to get advice on what to do."

I got up from my chair and walked over to my Keurig. I started another cup, Dark Jungle Blend. The sound of the machine spitting extra strong coffee into my mug sounded louder than it should have in the room fat with silence.

"Stefia, you know I'm going to tell you not to have an abortion," I said, taking the mug, and raising it to my lips. "You know that's my job, right?"

"Maybe you could try stepping away from your job. Maybe you could try saying something other than what people expect you to say."

"You almost sound like you want me to tell you that you *should* abort the baby..." I sipped carefully at the edge of the mug.

"No. That's not what I want. I just want someone to be honest with me and say what they really think. That's why I came here, Pastor. I want the truth, not some scripted answer. I figured I could trust you for the truth..."

"I am telling you the truth!" I said, passion filling my mouth as I set the mug down on my desk. "Stefia, abortion is wrong. That baby is God's creation..."

"That baby was put there by a man, not God," Stefia shot back. "Why in the world would God want me to have a baby?"

"Why are you playing devil's advocate?"

"It's how I know what the right decision is."

266

"God sees something for you that you can't possibly see yet. I believe that God chooses the best parents for each child…"

"Pastor, really?" She stood up from her chair, raising her voice. "You're going to use that line?"

"Stefia, it's the truth that I believe…"

"Seriously? I mean…seriously, Pastor Walt? My mother left when I was thirteen. You *know* that. And you've seen that now my father is completely hollow and unattached. My sisters and I were baggage to them. So don't tell me God chooses the right parents. Don't give me some line about how we get the parents we were supposed to have…"

"Stefia, you have a choice! We can all make choices. Your mother chose to leave. You can choose to not be like your mother! Stay with what God has given you!"

She shook her head, in frustration or disbelief, I wasn't sure. She leaned back in her chair and her eyes fell in line with the inspirational poster I'd thumb tacked to the ceiling two months earlier.

Strive not to be a success, but rather to be of value. —Albert Einstein

She closed her eyes.

"Have you ever thought that maybe God makes mistakes?" she asked.

"No. I have never thought that. I think that God challenges us. I think God stretches us. But I don't think He ever makes mistakes."

She still hadn't opened her eyes. With her head settled on the back of the chair, she jutted out her chin and tipped her head to one side and then the other.

Pop.

Pop.

Pop.

I shuddered. I hated it when people cracked their neck.

"You said you haven't told the father yet, right?" I asked, taking a seat.

"Yeah," she answered.

"How do you think he's going to react?"

"He will be angry."

"Why do you say that? How do you know?"

"I just know."

She opened her eyes and they scanned the room. She focused on the jade plant that sat on my window ledge, a malachite gem against the vast chalky whiteness of the snow outside.

"Was this relationship...?" I stopped, carefully choosing the words for what I wanted to know. "I mean, have you been together long?"

"It wasn't a one night stand," she said, with a razor sharp edge to her voice.

"I'm sorry. I didn't mean to offend you. It's just that...well, to be honest, I didn't think you had a boyfriend. I mean, I've never seen you with anyone."

"Surely you must realize, Pastor, that I don't live my *entire* life on stage."

"Touché."

I tried not to wonder, but couldn't stop my vagrant mind from land loping to who the father might be. Was it someone in our church? Someone outside the community? A fellow actor?

"Regardless of who this guy is that you've been with for...how long have you been together?"

"Long enough," she answered.

"Okay, regardless of who it is..."

"I'm not telling you who it is."

"I'm not *asking* you to. What I'm saying is that people have a way of surprising us, Stefia. Human beings are unpredictable and oftentimes react differently than we

269

expect. Honestly, I've counseled so many people in the church who have gone through this same thing."

"This same thing?"

"Yes, Stefia. The same exact thing. The reality is that unexpected pregnancies happen all the time..."

"This *same* thing?"

It was like she was stuck on the phrase.

"Stefia, whether we like to admit it, we're all the same. We try to make our situations different, for whatever reason, but really...we're all the same."

"I guarantee you, this situation is different."

"Why?"

"I can't tell you that."

"Is this a game, Stefia?"

There was so much being said. Her unwillingness to speak was saying more than the thing she wasn't saying.

Too bad I couldn't figure out what it was.

"Babies are a gift from God," I said. "And I would be willing to bet my reputation that this boyfriend of yours will step up and be the man God wants him to be. He may be surprised, Stefia, but if he loves you..."

"It's not love, pastor," she said. "I don't mean to be philosophical but I wouldn't describe it as love. And I wouldn't necessarily call him my boyfriend."

"So it's not a good relationship, then?"

"It's a complicated relationship. I don't know if it is good or bad."

"Stefia, I'm feeling like maybe I need to be worried about you. Is there something else that we should be talking about?"

"I assure you, there is no need to worry. This man and I...we have a history together. And he is, quite literally, why I have all that I have."

"Including," I said, derailing her philosophical tirade, "the baby in your belly." I couldn't handle anymore teasing or enigmatic answers. If she couldn't answer, I would stop asking.

She ran her fingers through her hair, massaging her scalp. I tried not to drive myself crazy wondering who else it was that had done that for her.

"I'll pray for you," I finally said. Because I would. I would pray for her.

But something sour churned in my gut because I knew I'd said it simply because I didn't know what else to say.

There was a quiet knock at the door, and then it opened just a crack.

"Pastor Walter?"

It was my secretary, and I'd never been more thankful for an intrusion.

"Your three 'o clock is waiting for you," she said. "Do you want me to tell them to come back?"

"No," I said, standing up and smoothing my khaki slacks. "Send them down."

She closed the door quietly, and I turned back to Stefia with an apologetic look.

"Looks like our conversation is over," she said.

I nodded, and she rose.

"Stefia, I'm not going to judge you," I said. "Only you can make this decision. But I know you. I know your heart. I know that you will choose the right thing."

"I know what's right, Pastor," she said. "I knew before I got here. I just wanted to talk to someone about it."

"Everything will be okay," I said, opening the office door for her. "I promise. You will get through this."

"It's just like a new show, right? Like...another performance. Come one, come all to see *Stefia and the Baby*..."

"I'm sure you're in for a standing ovation," I smirked.

"Yeah," she said, with a grin. "Maybe."

**

People are expecting words of wisdom. People are expecting me to approach the pulpit and recite some pat answer for how there is a reason for everything and God doesn't make mistakes and we will all get through this, let us pray, amen.

And I don't know what to say.

I've been praying for the right words. But the boxed up answers, the usual verses, the assurance that the people desperately crave that life is going to be okay isn't there this time.

I don't know what to say.

Sometimes we make the words so complicated. We rely on the fancy phrases. The things we're supposed to say. The things people are accustomed to hearing.

But sometimes people need to hear the truth.

I wish I would have said something different when Stefia sat across from me in my office. I wish I wouldn't have blathered on about how talented she was or how much everyone loved her. Why did I say all the same things everyone else had told her forever? She could have heard that from anyone.

273

But she came to me.

I should have said she mattered because she was a child of God.

I should have said she mattered because God loved her.

I should have said the things she did or didn't do made no difference.

No.

What I should have simply said was that she mattered. Not because she'd helped build a theater in a tiny town. Not because she was beautiful. Not because people would admire her for keeping the baby and doing the right thing. I should have told her she mattered, just because she did. Because everyone matters. Any person above her on the ladder of fame and every person she might have stepped on during her climb to the top. Every person who died on that stage with her down to the person who mopped up the blood and patched up the bullet holes. They all matter.

Just because they do.

The truth. That's what Stefia wanted to hear from me. Not the nicely packaged thing that looks like truth, but the real truth. The sour one that stings and screams and bleeds.

Perhaps that's what the people sitting in the sanctuary need to hear. Not that life is great and that God is good. What they need to hear is that, more often than not, life stings and burns and knocks out your front teeth. Life begs you to keep going while It ties your laces together and throws sand in your eyes. And yes, God is there, God is always there.

But that doesn't mean the sand in your eyes doesn't sting. It doesn't mean you won't trip over your laces.

Things need to be acknowledged. People's pain. People's mistakes. We need to stop washing over it all with a milky film that blurs our vision and messes up our path.

So why don't we?

Why don't we tell the truth?

I'll tell you why.

Because the real truth is there were not just six souls that were taken in the tragedy at the theater, there were seven. And somehow when Stefia gave me the power of knowing that, she took away my desire to say anything about it. Now I am bound by a truth that only I know.

Dear Lord, I must respectfully disagree with you. Because in this particular instance, knowing the truth has *not* set me free.

-Gage-

I once read a book that focused on how life's smallest decisions can have the longest lasting effects. It's ironic; huge earth shattering events starting with one seemingly insignificant choice.

Decisions matter. Every single one of them. Don't let anyone tell you they don't.

On a gut level, I think we know this—that the big things are made up of little things and that every choice affects something else. And yet we can't make that our focus. We can't let it paralyze us into not being able to make a decision at all.

Mindy and I had been dating for five months. We had a Thursday night off together—a rare occurrence for the horrific work schedules we kept—and we planned a special night out. I asked where she wanted to go and she surprised me by answering opening night of *What You Can't See* at the Crystal Plains Theater.

"A show?" I asked. "At Crystal Plains?"

"You don't like theater?"

It's not that I didn't like theater. I liked theater just fine. I just wasn't a fan of Granite Ledge. I decided not to tell her that—because decisions matter—and bought tickets for the upcoming show.

At 5:30 that Thursday night, I knocked on her door. She giggled like a schoolgirl at the sight of me standing on her front step holding a rose.

"You know, you don't have to knock on my door. You can just come in."

I smirked and handed her the flower.

"But," she said, taking the bloom and pulling it to her nose, "you can bring me one of these anytime."

She coiled her arms around my waist, hitting the butt of my gun. Her lips turned down in a disappointment that she was getting lazy about hiding.

"Do you have to bring that with?"

It wasn't that I had to. It was that I never went anywhere without it. Habit, I guess.

"We're not heading to the big city, Gage. It's Granite Ledge. Population, like, ten people."

She kept her arms around me but the snuggle loosened as she searched my face for some clue I'd take the gun off. But decisions matter and I didn't want to lie.

"Mindy, I'm allowed to carry. So I do."

I carried because decisions matter.

**

I'd scored pretty fabulous last minute tickets because of someone else's cancellation so we found ourselves watching the show from the second row of seats. We settled into the crimson colored upholstered chairs that looked as though they'd been stolen from an old movie theater. Mindy set her purse between her feet and paged through the program the ushers had handed out.

"Aw, I love this!" she said, pointing to one of the pages. "It's such a nice touch when they put the actors' headshots in the program. It's kind of neat to see what they look like in real life."

I wasn't going to look through it. I could have cared less what any of them looked like offstage, but out of some desperate desire to seem interested in things that mattered to my date, I decided to page through.

The smallest decisions set the largest events in action.

I saw her there, a face staring back from a black and white photo meant to appear spontaneous but obviously posed and well paid for. Her lips were parted perfectly, her hair falling in wisps around her face...and those eyes. I'd remember those bottomless but impenetrable eyes anywhere.

I shook my head, wanting to believe it could have been a twin. It could have been a doppelganger. It could have been my head playing tricks on me. But then I saw her name—Stefia Lenae Krist—and I knew.

And I remembered.

Because decisions always matter.

**

Two years earlier, I was six months in on my first job as a cop. I knew my position with the Granite Ledge department wasn't permanent. I had been waiting for a job to open up with Becker County where I was originally from. But I needed the experience and the money so Granite Ledge was as good a place to start as any.

It must have been October of that year; the sharp air caused locals to predict an unusually cold winter headed our way. I remember the crunch of leaves as I walked from my squad up to her house. The door rasped when she quickly pushed it open to meet me, her eyes huge and anxious.

"Oh my god, did something happen to dad?" she asked.

"No, no. Everything is fine," I said, noting the fear on her face. "I'm here to ask you a few questions. Can I come in?"

She pushed the door open the rest of the way so I could step inside and immediately invited me to sit at the dining room table.

"God," she said, as she sat down across from me, "when I first saw you pull up I was sure dad had been in an accident. Then when you said questions…wait, is this something about my mom?"

"Your parents aren't here, then, I take it?"

The report that had been filed said Stefia was fifteen. She didn't look fifteen. I knew that blessing was probably a double edged sword to live with.

"Dad is at work," she said, moving several scattered papers into a pile at the end of the table. "He leaves at 5:30 am and gets home about 7:30 pm. We don't see him a lot."

"And your mom?"

"Moved out a year or so ago."

She repeatedly squared up the papers, matching the corners and gently bumping the pile against the table like a deck of cards she was ready to deal out.

"Oh," I said. "I'm here to ask you some questions about a…" I flipped open the notepad I had in my shirt pocket. "Niles Connelly? He's your…"

"Neighbor," she finished.

"And…anything else?"

"He's the owner of the theater I work at."

I tapped a pen at my notebook. "I'm here to ask you about your relationship."

"My relationship…with Niles?"

**

The house lights dimmed and a hush settled over the audience like a blanket. Mindy reached over and took my hand. I wished I had popcorn. Or a beer. I kind of wished I was anywhere else.

And yet, there was something magical about an audience awaiting a show. You could feel the energy, like a thread of anticipation weaved throughout the people wanting to be entertained.

Show me something.

Show me something worth it.

Music began from the orchestra pit just ahead of us and it occurred to me that I knew little regarding the show we were about to see. I hadn't asked anything about it when Mindy announced she wanted to go, nor had I read anything online when reserving tickets. Mindy had only said it was an intense show that I'd enjoy.

"You know, because you're intense," she had said.

"Am I?"

I didn't really think I was intense. I thought of myself more black and white. Logical. Matter-of-fact.

"You're one way or the other," Mindy explained. "There's nothing wishy-washy about you. And that's intense."

I had smirked at her then, just like I smirked at her as she sat next to me, giddy like a little kid waiting for the curtain to open.

Things looked different from the second row. The actors moved across the stage so closely I could have reached out to touch them. I could see the microphones wound into their wigs and the powder used to set their stage makeup. I could even see the mist coming from their mouths as they delivered lines. Things looked so different up close and I soon found myself lost in a bubble of spit I saw hanging on the lead actor's lips.

And then Stefia appeared.

She snaked across the stage in a simple red dress, the shortness of the hem accentuated by red stilettos she must have taken lessons on how to walk in. She pivoted on the balls of her feet like she'd switched directions on a catwalk, then she stopped to stare at the actor she shared center stage with. Did she know the eyes of every man in the audience were traveling the length of her legs, willing the edge of her dress to jack up higher?

Mindy playfully smacked my thigh and I realized my mouth was hanging open so far it looked like my jaw had come unhinged. I squeezed her thigh and gave a quick smile.

"She's too young for you," Mindy jokingly admonished in a whisper.

The way she looked had nothing to do with my mouth hitting the floor. I was surprised simply for the fact it was *her*.

She had to be a senior by now—seventeen? eighteen?—but even without seeing her headshot in the program I would have known it was her. It was those eyes. The ones that had stared at me from across the dining room table that October. The ones that had questioned and gotten angry.

**

"Did Elliot put you up to this?" she had asked on that afternoon two years ago. Her question stabbed sharply at the thick air.

"I can't tell you who filed the report."

"You don't even *have* to tell me who it was. I know who it was. Who else would make up such a stupid story?"

I set my jaw and fixed my eyes in an unemotional stare.

"It's amazing what a guy will do when he's a little jealous, right?" she said. "I can't believe he went to you guys with this made up crap…"

She slammed the papers down on the table, undoing the perfect pile she'd spent the length of our conversation creating. She was so angry at whoever Elliot was that I almost wanted to defend him and let her know it wasn't even a guy who had filed the report. It was a classmate who had moved to town the year before and claimed she'd seen a much older man kissing Stefia in an old green Cutlass after school. She'd played detective and supposedly tracked the vehicle to Stefia's neighbor, Niles Connely.

Stefia continued on her tirade against Elliot and was close to convincing me everything between her and Niles was perfectly innocent. An actress of the finest measure, she might have distracted many well-meaning questioners with her witty responses and a flip of her hair. Most people would have easily believed there was nothing going on. And I might have believed her too, if it weren't for her eyes.

I've seen and heard a lot of strange things in my job—unbelievable things. You spend enough time on the darker side of life and pretty soon you naturally seek out the explanations that most people don't realize exist. I was carefully aware of the squint in her eyes as she spoke, the abstract anger she hurled around the room. It all told me something else was going on and that she had firmly decided not to say a word about it.

Decisions matter, and I can't help people who don't want to be helped.

Did I believe her? No. But it really didn't matter either way. Police work often doesn't pan out like in the movies. We don't sneak around and search for clues. We can't just pretend we have a reason for wanting to know or being somewhere we shouldn't be. More often than not, if the cards don't line up, there is simply nothing we can do. If Stefia wouldn't say anything, I had to move on.

And no matter how hard I tried, she wouldn't say a thing.

But then the victim almost never does.

**

Stefia continued her parade around the stage, now in a more conservative costume, angry at something another actor had said to her character. I'd missed the exchange while my mind wandered, and I worked to get back into the plotline of the play.

"You don't have a clue," Stefia bawled across the stage. "You don't know anything about what's going on…"

"How can I know if you won't tell me?" her fellow actor spit back. He pounced at her, taking both wrists and shaking her.

God, how often I'd felt that way when talking to the victim. I wanted to shake them. Slap them. Grab them by the face and push their lips open.

Why can't you just tell me?

Open up and say something.

The world is so full of noise and yet void of the things that need to be said. And as Stefia regurgitated lines that someone else had written down, I couldn't help but wonder if the stage was where she finally got out the things she needed to say without the commitment of having admitted them.

They were just lines, right? She was only reading lines.

Some might have said I was over-analyzing the situation. Others might have thought it was just part of being a cop and looking deeper than I needed to. I called it being careful. Paying attention. Not being fooled twice.

Not that she'd fooled me the first time. Like I said, I'd guessed as I sat across from her at the dining room table that afternoon that she wasn't telling the full story. But six months later at Beidermann's completely confirmed it.

At least it did for me.

I'd been hired at Becker County as their newest deputy and Chief Randall decided a shake at Beidermann's was an appropriate send off. So after I signed off as an officer with Granite Ledge for the last time, I met Randall in the parking lot of Beidermann's.

"I hate to see you go, kid," he said as we waited in line at the outdoor counter. It was unusually warm for April and I was looking forward to the cool ice cream sliding down my throat.

"Thanks, Chief."

"But I know Becker is where you really wanted to work," he continued. "I'm glad they hired you. They're getting a fine addition to their department."

He slapped me on the shoulder and turned to place our order.

"Two banana split shakes," he told the girl behind counter, and handed her cash to pay.

Chief Randall then made small talk with the girl who whipped up our shakes, something about a surgery the girl's mother had scheduled for the following week. I politely nodded along to their conversation, but found myself distracted by the old green Cutlass that had pulled into the parking lot.

The driver's side door opened and a tall and distinguished looking gent who I guessed to be in his late 40s stepped out. He dressed as though he didn't belong in small town Minnesota; his perfectly tailored skinny slacked suit gave him the appearance of someone merely passing through, possibly lost.

Ah. Niles Connelly, the eccentric and wealthy part owner of the Crystal Plains Theater. He walked around to the other side of the car and leaned down to his passenger through the open window. He flashed a dazzling smile at whoever sat there, then walked towards the outdoor counter to place his order.

Paying no attention whatsoever to the conversation Chief Randall was having, I slowly moved away from the counter to get a better look at who was sitting in the passenger seat. When my suspicions were confirmed, I casually moved towards the car, approaching it from the back bumper.

"Gosh, Niles," Stefia said when she sensed me coming up by her window. "You're always so fast."

Then she looked up from where she sat.

Two things happened at exactly the same moment. One of them was that Stefia realized I wasn't Niles. The second was that I noticed Stefia's skirt was cinched up on her left leg—so high that I could see the turquoise colored lace on the edge of her panties.

"Just your neighbor?" I said, watching her fingers clasp at the hem of her skirt as she slowly pulled down the fabric to cover her thigh.

She stared straight ahead out the windshield like I wasn't even there. I put my hand on the roof of the Cutlass and bent down so she could see my face.

"You know, you might be fooling a lot of people," I whispered into the car, "but for the record you have never fooled me."

She continued staring straight ahead, keeping her breath constant and measured.

"So, Stefia Lenae Krist, I'm gonna ask you one more time if there is anything you want to tell me."

She turned from the windshield and looked right at my face with those bottomless eyes.

"He's just my neighbor."

I blinked.

"And," she continued, "the owner of the theater I work at."

"Bullshit," I hissed into the car.

"Yeah? Prove it."

And then she smiled because she knew I couldn't.

**

The performance continued on stage in front of us, but I'd spent so much time in flashbacks I wasn't even sure what the storyline was that I'd paid sixty bucks for Mindy and I to see.

It almost didn't matter.

"You can't prove what you can't see," Stefia said to another actor on stage.

It almost didn't matter because it was as if the lines she recited in the play were delivered with perfect timing to the disgusting nostalgia in my head. Questions about everything I'd done or failed to do stabbed at my brain as my stomach worked itself into a giant knot. My armpits wept with perspiration like it was July, not February, and a warm twinge of nausea pricked at the top of my throat. I shifted uncomfortably in my seat, trying not to be a distraction.

"What's wrong?" Mindy whispered.

It obviously wasn't working

"I don't feel well at all," I said, swallowing hard. "I need to sneak out for a bit."

She nodded and I left as quietly as possible, whispering apologies to a few patrons who didn't bother to hide their annoyance. An usher standing at the doors pointed the way through the lobby to the restrooms.

I ran water in one of the sinks until it was icy cold and then cupped my hands under the stream. I lowered my face into the puddle I held in my palms, a soothing chill enveloping my head.

The mirror reflected a pale face back to me.

**

What do you do when people won't say anything? What *can* you do?

I was only eleven when I had woke early that morning to hear mom crying in her room. Nameless Boyfriend Number Six had just left, but not before screaming obscenities and cracking mom's face against the nightstand.

I wanted to help her. My god, the frustration of standing over her how many times as she bled into the carpet, the helplessness of hearing, "Don't tell anyone, Gage. He didn't mean to." I couldn't fathom her slipping away, moment by moment, year by year, and knowing all she had to do was speak up. Tell somebody. Make an admission.

At fifteen, I rested my hand on top of my mother's closed casket and spit out guilt and frustration at her defeated body that had been beaten lifeless for no other reason than she'd believed her lips were sewn shut. I had tried to make things better. I had tried to help my mother, but it was like watching a shadow bind a piano wire around her throat while she believed she had no hands to pull it off. I couldn't open her mouth for her. I could not reach down her throat and pull the words out. I couldn't help her.

Maybe that's why I became a cop. In some naive corner of my head I believed that some victim somewhere would be saved if I just walked in and said, "Tell him to stop!" It

291

hadn't worked for my mother, but maybe it was because I had started too late. If I got there quicker…if I started earlier…I was going to empower someone. I was going to save someone's life.

The longer I was a cop, the more I realized that superhero *I'm going to change the world* fairy tale was a joke. You couldn't help every person. Shit, you couldn't help *most* people. There were an infinite number of souls who slipped through the cracks because of their own decisions, and that's just the way it was.

**

I checked the men's room mirror again, desperately hoping for a darker shade of pale than when I'd first splashed my face.

And then I heard it. Screaming from somewhere outside the bathroom.

I pulled open the restroom door and the chaotic discord swelled. They were not squeals of delight in reaction to a stage effect, nor were they cries of surprise or awe. No, this wailing was primal. A collective howl of frantic voices that pricked something raw at the base of my neck.

Something was wrong inside the theater.

I picked up my step, headed for the door to the audience, my head electric and alive with synapses firing in preparation for whatever was happening inside.

And then I heard it. A gunshot.

And then another one. Another gunshot.

The average reaction time for a cop is 2.2 seconds. It's immediate. It was the entire reason we trained. I couldn't tell you how many situations I'd been in where my brain quickly processed I should grab for my gun, and I looked down to find it was already in my hand.

Another gunshot. And another one.

Shit.

I hated Granite Ledge.

Before I reached the door of the theater, it slammed open, a crowd of patrons spilling into the lobby. They screamed in disjointed, short breathed phrases I couldn't string together.

"The shooter?" I questioned one man. "Where is the shooting coming from?"

"Stage," was all he could choke out.

Shit.

Slowly pulling open the theater door and slipping inside, I probed my way into the dark audience. Always aware of my back, my feet, my head, where my gun was pointed, the crying from behind me as I crept forward in the aisle.

Taking shelter behind a ledge, I craned my neck to see ahead. In the stage lights still lit, I could see three bodies lying on stage, blood leaking into puddles around them.

I hated Granite Ledge.

My eyes darted across the stage; I needed to identify the shooter. I needed to find my target.

An actor who appeared to have already been shot once limped across the stage cradling his bleeding, broken arm and called out, "You don't mean to...you don't want to..." before a second bullet ripped through his face.

And then, I saw my target.

Shit.

A woman nearby, frantic at hearing another shot fired, hurled herself closer to me. She grabbed at the waist of my pants, setting all her weight near my midsection as though she was trying to climb over me to safety.

"Keep your head down!" I hissed, pushing her face towards the floor. Then I moved with calculated starts and stops, slinking my way from aisle to aisle, hiding behind chairs until finally I made it to the quarter wall near the orchestra pit. There was too much happening on stage for anyone up there to realize that's where I was headed.

But I couldn't screw it up. I needed a good shot. It wasn't like Hollywood. In Hollywood the perfect shot presented itself, the hero took it, the music swelled and the credits rolled. In real life, civilians stood up, got in the way, chaos erupted and the good guy lost sight of where he had aimed.

I needed a good shot.

We trained for how to make split second decisions—because every decision mattered. I racked my brain for all the black and white, logical, no nonsense training I'd sat through since before I'd even worked an actual day on the street. It was all there in my brain. I needed each piece of it now.

Out of the corner of my eye, I saw something move within the curtain fabric on stage. Someone was hiding inside it. I could see the bottoms of their shoes; I could tell it was a woman from the glossy white leather flats. I wanted to get to her. To tell her to stop moving. To stand still so she wasn't seen. I wanted to tell her...

Pop.

Pop.

Pop.

Within seconds, the young woman body's slumped to the floor, the white lace from her costume slowly turning as red as the curtain she'd tried to hide behind.

In training they tell you that once you have identified the suspect in a mass shooting situation, you don't negotiate. It's not like the movies. You don't try to talk to them. You don't try reasoning. You see them and you take them out.

Finish.

Them.

Off.

I turned.

I had my shot.

I took aim.

But there's a millisecond there to think. There's a minuscule fraction of a moment for something to go through your mind. And my last thought before I squeezed my trigger three times was that all the training in the world would never have prepared me for Stefia, with her impenetrable eyes, being the one I'd have to shoot.

-Stefia-

There is magic within the molecules of theater air. It is easier to breathe. Each gasp fills your lungs to bursting; your brain springs alive with the tingle of unleashed creativity.

Theater animates you. It grows you. Theater helps you know you exist.

If real life were like theater, you would write the script. You could choose your setting and your props. If a mistake was made, you could start over.

Take a break.

Run the scene again.

If someone would have handed me that evening as a script, it would have been easier. If someone could have blocked the scene, I'd have known what to do. If I could have been directed where to put my hand and turn my face when his eyes questioned me, how to react when Niles asked if something was wrong, the moment would have been beautiful. But instead I heaved, retching out the news like it was poison.

"Pregnant?" he said slowly, like the word was sticky on his lips. He combed the fingers of one hand through his hair, blurting out something like a laugh.

I forced my lips to bend into a smile. It was a pathetic attempt.

"Wait. You're serious?" he asked. "You're for real?"

"For real."

I couldn't read him. I couldn't tell what he was thinking. He sat up from his reclined position on the couch and sucked air through his closed teeth; it sounded like a leaky tire, only the air was going the wrong way. A volatile stillness crept into the house. It was so quiet all I could hear was the bubbler on the exotic fish tank in Niles' office.

"How long have you known?"

"Long enough."

He kept his face guarded. He grazed the pad of his thumb back and forth across the leather of the couch we sat on and focused so hard on the window above us I thought he was trying to separate the panes of glass in his vision.

By all rights, it should have been a lovely scene—the warm glow of the fireplace reflecting off the red of the couch, the clink of two ice cubes in his snifter of brandy, sultry jazz standards playing through his iPod. It was how I would have planned the scenery if it were up to me to write the scene.

But it wasn't up to me to write it, and it wasn't a lovely scene. I stood from the couch and moved towards the fireplace, fingering the framed publicity shots he'd crammed like trophies on his mantle.

"So, then," I breathed out. "What are you thinking?"

Niles sat on the edge of the couch, elbows on his knees with his hands cupped around his snifter.

"I'm thinking *darling, the things we go through together...*"

I put my hands out in front of the fireplace, soaking up the compassionate heat of the flames in my palms.

"I'm also thinking," he said, rising from the couch, "that I need more brandy."

He padded to the kitchen to half fill his glass, and then poked his head back around the corner.

"You want some?" he asked.

"Want some what?"

"Brandy."

I stared at him, unsure of why he would offer.

"No?" he said. "Just me, then. Okay."

My news had lit his nerves and complicated his behavior. He took a sip of brandy and set what was left on the mantle. He stood next to me and watched the flames etch into the cedar log that filled the room with the smell of woody goodness.

"So," I started, wishing again that I had a script to follow.

"Yes?"

"Niles, what are we going to do?"

His steely eyes searched mine. Maybe he was hoping I would answer my own question. Then he slowly pulled me into his chest and kissed the top of my head. He wrapped his arms around me, keeping his chin settled in my hair.

"Now, Stefia," he said. "You know we can get through this, right?"

I settled my face on his chest and nestled into the scent of him. I breathed in who he was; older, wiser, warmer. My head spun in circles coming to terms with the idea that part of that—part of him—lived within me now.

Pastor Walter was right. Everything was going to be okay. Why had I second guessed it? Why had I doubted at all?

The embrace Niles held me in swayed ever so slightly, and when I looked up into his eyes, his lips played out what I could only describe as a serious smile. I knew it was not the alcohol causing him to rock; his tolerance was much higher than what he'd sipped on that night. No, the movement was actually an invitation to dance. And so we swayed in time to Ella Fitzgerald's *Someone To Watch Over Me* and the snap of the cedar log in the fireplace.

It was beautiful. And for that single breath of perfection, I was glad I hadn't written the scene of how the night would go because I never would have captured it with such restoring grace.

The song ended, signaling our dance was over and Niles gave a sweeping bow. And I didn't yet know it, but he'd disarmed me by the upturn at the corner of his mouth, all the while keeping something hidden behind his eyes.

He grabbed for another sip of his brandy and then patted at his pockets like he was searching for car keys. Finding nothing, he stepped to the kitchen, checked the top of the refrigerator, and found what he was looking for.

His wallet.

He opened it and set five crisp hundred dollar bills on the mantle, fanning them out where they laid.

"That should be enough to take care of it," he said. "If not, let me know."

My mouth went dry.

"Take care of it?" I asked.

He swallowed his last sip of brandy.

"Let yourself out," he said, kissing my forehead. "Okay?"

Then he walked up to his bedroom with his empty snifter and quietly closed his door.

**

We didn't talk for two weeks. I went to rehearsal as normal, but he stayed away from the theater. I knew we needed to clear the air—opening night was only a week away. So on a chilly evening after rehearsal, I called him from the theater and said my car wouldn't start and I needed a ride. He showed up fifteen minutes later and found me sitting alone on the edge of the stage.

"No one else could drive you home?" he asked, blowing the chill from his hands.

"My car is fine. I wanted to talk to you."

"I figured as much."

"Here," I said, sliding off the stage to place a coiled wad of cash in his hand.

He eyed me curiously, and then counted the money.

"But…this is five hundred dollars."

"Were you expecting change?" I asked.

"I wasn't expecting you to bring me anything back."

"I didn't need the money."

"You paid for it yourself?"

"No," I said. "I'm not having an abortion."

He didn't smile. He didn't laugh. He didn't move a muscle.

"Tell me you are joking, Stefia."

"I could," I said, rubbing at my elbow in a nervous habit, "but then I'd be lying."

"This isn't funny."

"I didn't mean for it to be."

He slapped his hand up to the winter hat still on his head and ripped it off in one swoop.

"Damn it, Stefia, don't do this!" He balled up the hat and tossed it at the ground. "You'll ruin your future. You'll ruin this theater."

"This theater?" I laughed. "How does me keeping a baby ruin this building?"

"Not the building, the *theater*," he said, stressing the word to show I'd missed the difference. "We are the theater; don't you get that by now? My brains and money, your beauty and talent...you're just going to throw that away for a kid?"

"Trust me, Niles. I know what I'm doing."

"You have no goddamn clue what you're doing!"

His eyes spun wildly around the room, first up to the flies, then across the stage, then around him in the aisle. Dragging his hands through his hair and messing it up more than his hat already had, he exhaled forcefully and muttered something I didn't fully hear.

"What?"

"I said if you keep that kid, it's not mine."

If I would have written the script, I'd have known he was going to say that. I would have prepared a witty response to follow his line. But I hadn't written the script so his words were like a blade pulled from nowhere and twisted into my gut.

"No one will ever know it's yours..." I finally said, swallowing a hard, dry lump. But he wouldn't stop. Taking him out of the picture and removing his responsibility only further irritated the situation.

"You keep that kid and I guarantee you'll never work in any theater around here again," he said and scowled. His eyes glared with intensity and turned the skin of my face hot. "I know people, Stefia. I'll make sure you never make it on stage anywhere."

"Niles..."

"I'm not joking, Stefia. You can't keep this kid. You can't do theater with baggage. You can't..."

"Baggage?" I screamed. "You mean someone you care about?"

"I mean something that holds you back," he spit out. "Something you're putting before the theater. Something that distracts you..."

"You don't have anything holding you back? You don't have anything you're putting before the theater?"

"Nothing."

"Really, Niles?"

"Really."

"Then what am I?"

My question smothered the room in silence. Time seemed slow and fat, sloshing through like humidity, as I lingered for the answer Niles held on his lips.

"You, Stefia, are an amazingly talented, beautiful seventeen-year-old girl who fucked up."

I felt him at my center, cutting through the mess of everything that had tangled us together. His face was completely emotionless and hard as he deflected any blame that was his to take. He plucked his hat from where he'd thrown it and pulled it down over his ears. He adjusted his coat, pushing the collar up around his neck.

"You were not supposed to get attached. This is theater, Stefia."

He turned away from me to walk up the aisle.

"Niles, you're wrong," I called to him.

"About what?" He didn't even turn around.

"This isn't theater," I said. "This is real life."

**

That night, I didn't go home. I drove to the lot at Pine Tree Park and crunched my way through the snow to sit on a swing. Phone in hand, I started and erased eight texts to Elliot because he was the only person who came to mind when I realized I needed real help. But I didn't know how to ask for help from someone I'd spent the last four years pushing away. I didn't know if I even had the right to ask. After our blow-up in the theater parking lot in the fall, I wouldn't have been surprised if he'd never talk to me again.

Could use a friend. Know where I could find one?

I pressed send.

The sky was clear and the stars dotted the blackness I stared up at. They shone like minuscule spotlights onto the stage of the world, illuminating our performances, our dramas and tragedies and comedies.

Our mistakes.

Our failures.

With the swing cradling the backs of my thighs, I pumped my legs. The icy cold metal of the chains squeaked into the silence of early morning as I reached higher and higher with every forward thrust of my feet. If I could grab those stars, if I could pull them down and keep them in my pocket, I would have my own spotlight for whenever I needed it.

For whenever I decided to write the script.

My phone buzzed in my coat signaling a text message, and I stopped pumping, dragging my boots through the snow under the swing to stop. My head tingled with nervous anticipation as I fumbled for my phone to check what Elliot had written back.

Message unable to send.

I stared in disbelief at my phone, its low battery light flashing, and realized my fingers were too cold and numb to even press the button to shut it down. As I mindlessly shoved the phone back in my pocket, one thought passed through my mind: this is what it's like to feel completely alone.

The irony made me want to puke. To always feel watched but abandoned. To have everyone's eyes on you but feel as though there is no one to talk to. To sense that you're being followed, hounded, celebrated, and realize you're actually isolated.

This was the sardonic twist—that you could be completely solitary and not even know it.

The reality was that it was just me, myself, and I.

Well, and a baby.

And something told me it was time to write the script.

**

I took center stage. I knew the eyes of every man in the audience were soaking up the sight of my long legs in red stilettos, but I paid no attention. I was simply soaking up the warmth of the spotlight. It was an odd sort of logic to be comfortable in a bright light; you can't hide anything when it shines on you. But I wanted to be in that light forever. I wanted the hot, blinding magic to sizzle on my skin, like stars blazing from inside my pocket.

The spotlight turns you into a brilliant show of fireworks that begs others to watch. *Look at who I am*, you want to scream. *I can't hide. I'm right here.*

Dust floated in the spotlight beam, illuminating a pathway of glitter that led beyond where I could see. Was that like the bright light they always spoke of in near-death experiences?

Look at me.

Would I see a bright light?

People paid money to watch me on stage but they had always watched me, everywhere. They'd watched from the coffee counter or their lockers or from the street or spying in windows like they had bought a ticket to watch my life unfold, busting into corners they didn't belong in. Boundaries were drawn, erased, and scribbled over again, like a new set built for every performance I did.

Once you hit the stage, you never left it, even if you walked right off the edge.

Watching a show isn't the same. Once you've been on stage, you can't just warm a chair in the audience. That's a betrayal to your soul.

I get that now, Mother.

**

Four scenes later, we all tossed lines back and forth and I was glad to be in a more comfortable costume. My bag, slung across my body from one shoulder and resting on the opposite hip, was weighty. The handgun I'd snuck from Niles' collection and slipped inside was heavy but strikingly similar to the prop gun I was supposed to use at the end of the first act.

I was writing the script.

And since I was writing the script, I got to decide what people said. And the most important thing that I wanted everyone to say was that this was not a love story gone sour.

Repeat after me.

Read the lines.

This was not a love story gone sour. The way this all played out had nothing to do with Niles. Nothing at all. You see, this was—*always was*—about my mother. This was about not becoming her.

The thing is, as I had walked away from Niles' house that night with five hundred dollars shoved in the pocket of my jeans, I pondered my two options. The first was to have an abortion. I could take the money and drive to some city where they didn't know who I was. I could pay them to rid myself of the baggage, because there's no place for that in the theater.

Although Niles was the one who had said that, it was my mother who had proven it to me. There's no place for baggage in the theater.

Right, Mother? Leaving a kid in order to be on stage—*that's what we need to do.*

But abandoning the baby would make me just like my mother. And I would not be my mother.

So the other option was to have the baby, deal with the baggage, and live life without the theater. I thought on that one for a long time. I swirled it around in my head, feeling it sink like a brick to the center of who I was. And you know what I realized?

Genes run deep.

I know why my mom had to leave. I now knew what she meant in her letter under the tree that said *If ever you find something that makes you feel alive, chase after it and never give up.* Because now I know what it's like to look at the stage and feel like your life is slipping past if you're not on it. I know the addiction. I know the magnetism.

Which also made me like my mother.

And then, creeping up my throat like bile I couldn't swallow fast enough, came a third option. I didn't want to know life without the theater. I couldn't. But I wasn't going to have an abortion.

The third option—the only fair one—was to take us both out of the picture.

This time, I was writing the script.

**

My skin glistened with sweat. The gun in my hand was heavier, colder than the prop gun.

The first two shots were just for noise. The deafening pop and ring were infinitely different than the hollow short rap of the prop gun. Then the screaming began, rooting through my head like a worm burrowing into my ear. Shouts of individual names suffused with *it's a real gun* and chaos rippled through the audience like waves of nausea.

Carly was the first on stage to realize the gun was real. She turned to run and I shot, catching her through the ear. She spun and fell in a heap, like someone had dropped a giant sack of birdseed. She inhaled only twice more.

Erick just stood there, so full of fear he'd lost color in his face. I shot him. Then I shot Tony.

In rehearsal I'd watched them lay on the stage, trying to keep as still as possible without getting the giggles. But now they were motionless, growing pools of blood soaking through their costumes. I was horrified and mesmerized at the same time. Brownish, chocolately red puddles bloated from beneath their bodies; a color completely unlike the crayon a child grabs for bloodied fangs of a coloring book vampire.

If they'd followed the script I had in my head, Erick would have run at me. Tony would have got to me quicker. Someone would have stopped me.

Did I have to spell it out for everyone? Did I have to connect the dots for them?

I can't hide.

I'm right here.

Come stop me.

Don't you see? There is no pedestal here. It's just me. And I fucked up.

Come stop me.

Bobby had already been hit by the same bullet that took Tony, but the only thing that had been damaged was his arm. He slinked towards me, weak from the sight of the blood leaking down his arm.

"Stop," he pleaded with me. "You don't mean to do this. You don't want to…"

He was wrong. I had a part to play. I'd written a script in my head.

I pulled the trigger without flinching.

So much blood. Spatters joined with splotches, swelling into pools underneath the four people whose bodies were in various states of shut down. Amazement washed over me as I realized there was blood everywhere—like I had given birth, not taken life.

I almost missed it, but a glint of light revealed shiny white shoes hiding just off of stage right. Aubrey had hidden inside where the open curtain collected itself on the side of the stage. She wasn't stopping me. She was only trying to save herself. I shot into the curtain three times.

If my math was correct and I hadn't lost count, I needed to reload. I pulled the clip from the gun, tossed it aside, and slammed my hand into my bag for another one. But my hand got tangled inside, so I glanced down.

I heard three shots in quick succession before I felt them rip through my skin. The wind knocked out of me, I dropped my gun and fell sprawled out on stage. Instantly I was gurgling. Spitting. Gagging on blood.

I couldn't swallow.

I couldn't breathe.

But for that millisecond before my heart stopped, in that minuscule fraction of a moment before I died, I smiled.

Because someone had finally read my script.

You see, in the end we are only the stories that people tell about us.

So please tell the story about a girl who found herself in theater and pegged it to be her reason for living.

And tell the story about the same girl who found herself pregnant and refused to become her mom.

Please tell the story about a girl wouldn't leave her baby and instead chose to leave *with* her baby.

Because there is a difference.

There's *always* a difference between who we are and what they see.

❧

The Me You See is the third novel by Shay Ray Stevens.

You can find out more about Shay Ray, her books,

and the next project she has up her sleeve

by visiting her website,

shayraystevens.com

You can also connect with Shay Ray

via Twitter (@shayraystevens)

Facebook (facebook.com/shayraystevens)

or Pinterest (pinterest.com/shayraystevens).

Please consider leaving a review on Amazon.

Thanks!

❧

Made in the USA
Lexington, KY
22 August 2017